Joyce Stranger is the author of many well-loved novels for both adults and children, and animals figure prominently in all of them.

Although born in London, Joyce Stranger has always been closely involved with animals. She trains her dogs for obedience shows and spends much of her time walking them in the woods and fields, so that her sensitive portrayal of animals and the countryside is based on her own experiences and observation. She and her husband now live in a cottage in Anglesey with three dogs: golden retriever Janus, German shepherd Puma, and German shepherd Chita, and a Siamese cat called Chia.

# THE JANUARY QUEEN

Joyce Stranger

**CORGI BOOKS**
A DIVISION OF TRANSWORLD PUBLISHERS LTD

THE JANUARY QUEEN

A CORGI BOOK 0 552 11536 3

Originally published in Great Britain by Michael Joseph Ltd.

PUBLISHING HISTORY
Michael Joseph edition published 1979
Corgi edition published 1980

This book is set in 10 point Times Roman.

Corgi Books are published by
Transworld Publishers Ltd,
Century House, 61–63 Uxbridge Road,
Ealing, London W5 5SA

Printed and bound in Great Britain by
Cox & Wyman Ltd., Reading

Dedicated to my grandson
Jonathan
and my granddaughters
Mairi and Morag

# CHAPTER ONE
◆◆◆◆◆◆◆◆◀

It had been a bad week in a bad month in a bad year.

Charles Malone huddled into his anorak, pulling the fur collar and hood well round his face. His feet seemed not to belong to him. The ground was freezing. There was a full moon, high in the sky, the only good thing about the night. He could see clearly.

Behind him the rough stone wall gave little shelter. Beyond him his sheep lay, huddled out of the wind that cut with its bitter blast. There would be thick frost by morning. The ground was already hard, white glittering among the tussocks under the chilly light.

Frost alone was bad enough.

Some of the ewes might lamb tonight, and there were new young lambs in the field close to home. Next year he would install a lambing parlour. He wanted it now, but it was far from easy to get a builder. The good men were all busy, with work enough for years ahead, and he and his men had no time to spare. Here, not so far from the farmhouse, ten lambs had died in the last week. Ten newborn animals, brutally savaged before they were able to stand; and savaged, he was sure, not by a fox but by a dog. The fur caught on the barbed wire was blue-grey, not red.

He blew softly into his hands and cuddled his gun. He put his fur gloves on again. He would have to act swiftly, if the dog came. He needed help. He could not ask the men to stay all night; and he could not ask Kate, his daughter, to shoot a dog. He wished for the hundredth time that Tim, his son, had not left home. He had built the farm for Tim; had hoped the lad would inherit and take a pride in building as his father had built. He and Nell had worked every hour God made, had slaved from dawn till dark, had built the farm from nothing—from a derelict shambles, left behind by an old man who died, and who had kept on with his work long after common sense dictated he should have retired. There had been so much to do.

They had modernised and extended the farmhouse. Nell was little use outside, as she was not farmborn, but a city girl, met during the war, and married while bombs fell and the world went to hell, and the future was only a dream, perhaps never to be realised.

They had had a future, which now was their past. Nell was a genius in the house. They had inherited furniture from her mother and had been very glad of it. They needed all their money for the farm. It was heavy ugly stuff that Nell hated, but she had covered the vast chairs with bright covers, had created colour schemes that welcomed a tired man, had made a home. They had grown apart in many ways, but he could not do without Nell.

There was a whisper of wind, a sound of running paws, a movement among the huddled sheep, and then silence. The bitch at his feet moved too. She was warm and comforting, cuddled close against his legs. She lifted her muzzle and he put down a hand. Meg was more to him than almost any living creature; companion by day and by night on such watches; knowing every thought. A gradely bitch, old Tom the shepherd said, his Yorkshire ancestry uppermost. The best Charles had ever had. He took off his glove and buried his hand in the silky fur and Meg murmured to him, a soft growling sound as heartfelt as a purr from a cat.

If only Tim had been here beside him, but 'if only' was the most common phrase in the land. Tim was away, working as a farming journalist and doing well. His heart never had been in the farm; only in words on paper. He could speak the farm language and his pieces on new methods and new ways of working were becoming widely known. Charles was proud of his son, yet regretful too; it would have been good to have Tim at home to talk to; to discuss things with. Nell was busy all the time: shopping took hours as they were twelve miles from the nearest town, and the house took all her energy. It was big and inconvenient and she managed alone. The kitchen, which was big, friendly, and the room where everyone lived, was always in need of major cleaning. The men brought mud in and worse.

Nell often railed at them, but her complaints were not bitter—the men knew her tongue ran away with her, and that when they were in need of help, Nell would be the first to bring comfort. A sick wife; a baby in hospital; a man injured. She had nursed during the war and her skills were still remembered. She was asleep in her warm bed now. Lucky Nell.

He was cold. Visions of steaming mugs of cocoa danced in front of his eyes and he laughed at himself ruefully. The hell with this caper; why had he tied himself to a flock of sheep? Because the sheep were more important to him than almost anything else except the dog. He'd bought a new ram; he was sending Kate and Rob for it tomorrow. The thought of Rob irked him. The lad was a farm student, son of a friend, and he'd been doing Jack a favour. Too much of a favour as Kate and Rob had eyes only for each other. And Rob wasn't a worker. He was easy come, easy go, forgetting important things and neglecting vital precautions, with no sense at all. Yet he couldn't send Rob back—Jack Leicester was too good a friend to lose.

The farm paid well because he was wedded to it, as Nell often grumbled. Monday to Monday, weekends and weekdays, he was there, working, thinking, planning; looking at the ewes, picking out the best, his eye on prizes at the summer shows; on rams that would give him the best flock in the whole county; in the whole country. It was just such a ram that was due in the morning. He could see it in his mind, now. A fine upstanding noble beast; beautifully made, strong as they come, with a fleece on him that would put any other fleece to shame.

He had already paid and a fine price he'd paid; the highest ever paid for a ram in these parts. Everyone knew.

It had hit the farming headlines after the Auction. He looked out at the shadowy trees. The wind rustled in the branches; a dry cold sound; a bitter sound, a menacing sound, speaking of gales and snowfall and sheep hidden and lost. He must bring them all down to the home fields; they needed extra food anyway. The grass was rock hard and impossible to crop. They stood, hanghead and miserable, backs to the wind.

He needed his son beside him.

That was a useless thought. Tim had to go his own way. Charles had gone his own way. His father had bred horses—magnificent horses—and Charles loathed horses. His brothers all rode at the summer shows, one of them qualifying for top jumping until marriage put an end to his career. There was never money to spare after that, with five children to feed.

The old man had wanted Charles to ride; had put him on the back of one of the lively ones and made him mount again and again as he picked himself up. All that had done was to make him hate horses for ever and dodge riding whenever he could. He still hated horses and would have nothing to do with them, though Kate hankered for her own mare. She too had inherited the old man's passion. She could wait till she was away from home and earn the money for her own horse. Her father would never buy her one.

He looked again across the fields. The bushes and high walls that gave shelter to the sheep were black shadows in the night.

Nothing moved.

He glanced at his watch. The ebb of night; the hour of misery and death when men slipped slowly out of life. He would freeze here and nothing accomplished. But he had promised to watch. His farm was the fifth to be hit. The beast, whatever it was, had a pattern and the pattern indicated that it would hunt here tonight. His neighbours had each taken a turn. Now it was his turn.

He yawned and stifled the sound. The wind was dropping; if the night were still, nothing would carry his scent to the raider. The brute only came when darkness hid him from those who waited. He was sly; he was cunning; he was death on four paws; he was a killer without mercy.

There were other killers: men waiting behind hedges in darkness in other countries in the world, lurking as he lurked, but on even more brutal business. Man against man. Man against beast. Charles was falling asleep, he was growing maudlin, he was tired. God, he was tired. He yawned again, a wide mouth-cracking aching yawn that made the bitch at his feet yawn too. He grinned to himself, as she settled, nose on paws. She was comfort there in the night.

Charles might have been a million miles from home; cradled in space. He looked up, at the glimmering stars, thinking of men out there, unimaginably alone in the silence. It was bad enough here. How could a man endure that distance from the world, circling it endlessly, cooped in a fragile metal ball. The very thought was enough to bring on insanity.

He had to concentrate. It would be easy to sleep, to forget why he was here. He longed for his bed. Every muscle was protesting. His back was aching, his legs were cramped and he would never be able to pull the trigger. He took off his gloves and blew on his hands. Kate and Nell—both would be sound asleep. Lucky Kate. Lucky Nell. Lucky cows in the cowsheds; lucky folk in the dark houses huddled on the skyline, not a patch of light disturbing the blackness. The world had gone to sleep and left him on his own.

Damn the marauder. He hoped it was a fox. He loathed shooting a dog. A dog was a creature nearer to man than any other beast. People who had never had a dog—who did not know the companionship offered, the quality of devotion, the pleasure of training the callow pup till it was a wonderful adult, a man's right hand—they knew nothing.

An owl called, a long ghost call, a scream of misery in the night. Meg lifted her head and licked his wrist. She settled again, content to be with him, never complaining whatever he asked her, however unreasonable. She was more than his right hand and his legs; she could use her

11

brains to rescue a trapped lamb, to lead a ewe home when it strayed. She had more sense than any dog in the county. She felt his pride in her and leaned closer, warm against his steadily numbing leg.

She lay as if spilled on the grass, moonlight gleaming on her black and white body, on her head, white striped down the nose, white patched on one ear, a spark of white by one dark eye. She wore her ears pricked alert, knowing she was on duty. No matter what came, eagle or wolf or questing tiger, Meg would guard him and her sheep with her last breath. She meant too much to him to risk her against a dog gone wild.

It was colder than January, for all that it was mid March and the first daffodils were showing in Nell's rockery. The wind had stirred itself again, was growing fierce, was keening down the fields, sweeping the hillside above him, a wind from the Arctic, snow in its wake. The first thin flakes were drifting on the air.

It was all he needed now. He must find a builder to build that lambing shed; to keep his beasts safe from frost and from snow and from prowling fox and hunting dog. The killer ranged widely; ten miles in a night; he left telltales behind him. Sheep killed and half eaten, torn apart, mutilated, the fields bloody around them. It sickened him every time he saw it; the beasts he had lavished his skill on, torn and dying. Bloody and dead. It was probably a village dog. Why the devil couldn't people keep their dogs in?

They were pests, the straying dogs, all of them, packing, hunting, killing. Five thousand sheep and more died every year, thanks to stray dogs. Charles liked dogs, loved dogs. He hated the people who bought a pup and didn't care enough, and most of all he hated those who found the pup too much for them after a few days, because it was dirty, messy and they didn't know how to train, and then had it taken at only a few weeks old to be put down. He knew the Christmas story too well, and it wasn't the old, well-loved legend: 'The pup was a present, we can't do with it. Put it down.' He hated people, hated them more tonight when they were sleeping warm and uncaring and he was

12

out in the bitter cold, because of someone else's carelessness. He shifted position trying to keep warm.

He attempted to goad himself to alertness by thinking of the dead lambs, of more lambs dying, to keep his mood intact, to keep the anger flaring, to forget that this was a dog he was killing—perhaps a loved pet. He was at war with an enemy; no soldier could think of the man he shot as a man with friends and family, with babies to go home to, a wife to love him. Memories of bomber nights came back to him, clear nights like this, flying over Germany, looking down on sleeping houses, knowing that soon death would fall from the air, would tear and destroy and maim and kill. How could they ever have done it?

That was no thought to dwell on, not with death in his own fields and his profit at stake. He had the farm to run and a wife and daughter to feed, and men to pay. No time for pity. No room for mercy. Not only his lambs were at stake. Other farms had suffered too.

Last night Betsina had had a breach calf; the vet had to come, and that would be another big bill. No end to the expenses. He had three dry cows now, and a fourth had missed taking. He was going to abandon A.I. and go back to the bull. Nothing like the old ways. Maybe men had gone too far with their improvements. Nature kicked back hard.

He wished he could huddle up with the sheep. They'd run if he moved. They at least had warm fleeces. His own clothing was totally inadequate for standing still on a night like this. He could feel the icy stones of the wall behind him. The sheep were quiet shapes, huddled and still, used to the man and the dog. Till Meg came running among them, a fleet little shadow, slipping this way and that way, doing her job magnificently.

He was tired and bitterly cold and every irritation was magnified. He was cramped and he was angry. He moved first one leg and then the other, and tried to move his toes. He doubted if he had toes any more. It was perishing out here. He hated everybody at that moment. Tim, who had left him to farm alone and would never want the farm as an inheritance; Kate, who was sleeping peacefully and who

13

...t the moment so besotted about Rob that neither of ...m were any use. Kate needed to face reality. She was petted and spoiled and his darling, and he ought to harden his heart, but he never could and neither could Nell, though she was firmer than he.

No sleep tomorrow night either; the sow was due to farrow. She was the one sow that could never be left for a moment. Morwena always had problems—she felt the birth so slightly that she would stand and rub the emerging piglet against the wall, to quell an itch, and there he would find a dead baby instead of a live one; or she stretched herself blissfully after the birth, crushing half the litter. She was a pest and he didn't know why he endured her, but she bred good stock. It was worth the trouble, but two nights running spent awake, was two nights too many.

He would sell up and go and live in the Caribbean where the sun shone and it was warm and the blue sea whispered against the shore and a man had peace. No more animals. No more Meg. He poured coffee from the flask at his feet. Meg looked up at him, and he took the pack of sandwiches Nell had made him out of his pocket. He bit into ice cold bread, and then warmed the filling in his hand and fed it to the bitch. She sat, eager, eyes alight at the scent of meat.

Nothing like a picnic in the middle of the night in a deserted field with the temperature as low as it could go. It would soon be time for milking. The raider wasn't coming now. He'd be dead on his feet by morning. If only Nell could milk, but she had never done anything round the farm. She was far too busy running the house and feeding them all. He had one man sick and Rob would not be there. The boy had been born without a time sense.

The coffee scalded his tongue. He felt it flowing into him, warming him. It was hot and sweet and Nell had added a little rum. It was bliss, it was nectar, it was wonderful—the best thing in the world at this second, except for the thought of bed. Charles could forget that. He would not dare go to sleep, even if he went home now. He might as well stay on. He huddled down against the wall, and Meg leaned against him, warm against him, and he buried his face in the densest coat she had grown for years, hiding his ice-raw skin from the Arctic wind. There was nothing like a dog for company. She asked nothing, stood against him, waited for him to tell her their vigil was over.

There was a bleat on the hill, and then another. There was a panic running, the beat of hooves on the rock-hard ground, the crying of frantic animals. There was a restlessness among the beasts, a senseless milling, and then they took off, the herd racing in the far field. Meg was on her feet, waiting.

The dog was coming. It had to be a dog and not a fox. Meg was quivering with excitement and he put a hand on her scruff, holding her back. She was well trained, but instinct demanded that she run, that she meet menace with menace, that she fight. Charles didn't want her to fight. She was quivering and eager, desperate to be away, every muscle tense.

The clouds split apart and the moon shone full, lighting white fleecy backs and the small black heads of two new lambs. When had they come? They were early. Charles cursed; he should have been there. They should have been nearer home; lucky nothing had gone wrong.

The panic had spread and the sheep were running blindly, and lambs would be dropped, born dead. Meg was off, pulling away, knowing her job was to keep the sheep safe, flashing in among their white bodies, a twisting darting black and white dog, doing the job she'd been bred for and Charles didn't want her there. He couldn't shoot if she started to fight and fight she would.

The moon shone full on the intruder. A tall thin sheep dog, only one like it in the district—George Merry's blue merle and it wasn't a dog for Meg to tangle with. It was mean tempered, a surly brute, and always had been. Maybe it had a brain tumour. It was panicking the sheep now, driving them every way, and Meg was trying to get at it, her voice lifted in a sharp high bark that made the merle pause and glance towards the bitch, trying to identify the noise that menaced him. It *was* Sam, the dog from Granite Stack. There was no mistaking him now, and George was a neighbour and a friend. He liked his dog

15

though no one else did, but George would be the first to admit it had to go. There was no denying this evidence. There would be sheep inside the beast when they did the post mortem.

The blue merle turned towards Meg, determined to see her off. The man needed to shoot before the dogs met, but it was impossible to get a decent sighting through the sheep. The sound of fighting dogs came to him as he lifted the gun. There was a snap and a snarl and a worry and high squeal that could only be Meg. Charles was running, trying to work his way through the mêlée, and the sheep, too stupid to move out of the way, were impeding him. His heart was thundering, his breath was raw in his throat, the wind was bitter on his cheeks, his eyes were streaming with the cold, and his only guide was the snap and snarl and growl of the two dogs.

The blue merle sped towards the farmer at a loping gallop and he took quick aim and fired. It rolled and somersaulted and lay still. Meg had left her marks on the animal. Charles knelt to make sure it was dead, feeling hatred of himself and of the job he had to do in the morning, telling George.

Meg came back, tail wagging, carrying one paw high. It was a bad bite, but it would heal. Her master lifted her, holding her against him, ignoring the blood that marked his clothes. He wanted to reach home, into the warm, bathe his bitch's injuries. There was more than one bite on her, but she did not seem too much harmed. She licked his hand. He had forgotten the gun and went back for it, lifting it gently from the ground.

Charles covered the distance between the field and the farmhouse fast, and cursed under his breath as the back door swung from his frozen hands and slammed. He hadn't wanted to make a noise. The fire was out, but he switched on the fan blower, and laid Meg on the rug. She beat her tail again.

There were footsteps on the stairs. Nell came into the room, her eyes sleepy, tying the cord of her dressing gown.

'Did you get the dog?'

He nodded.

'It was George Merry's blue merle.'

Nell said nothing. She knew it would be unwise to speak. She busied herself with boiling the kettle, with putting warm water in a basin and bringing cotton wool and disinfectant and the syringe loaded with antibiotic, and then, as Charles began to bathe Meg's wounds, she put on milk to warm, mixing it with oatmeal, and brought it to the bitch.

Meg took the food greedily.

'She's been lucky,' Charles said. 'A few days' rest and she'll be fine. She did a grand job.'

'She always does.' Nell looked down at the little bitch. She wasn't overfond of dogs, but they had a way of making themselves part of the family and Meg lived with them. She stroked the shining fur on the bitch's skull and Meg wagged her tail again.

'You'd better have more coffee and a bite before you start milking,' Nell said, knowing Charles would never go back to bed now. 'Why don't you have a bath? It would warm you.'

It was a good idea, he thought, lying in warm water. It was a bad idea, he thought a moment later as feeling returned with a dazzle of pain to fingers and toes. He towelled himself vigorously, dressed in fresh clothing, and went down to find bacon and eggs and a mountain of fried bread ready to eat. Nell built the fire again, setting a match to it, to warm the bitterly cold room. They had never given up the open fire; it welcomed frozen men on chilly days and Nell liked the glow it brought to the hearth.

Charles ate, his mind on the day's jobs. Kate and Rob to fetch the ram. The milking to get through. He looked at Meg. She had curled into her basket, nose to tail and for a moment he was worried.

'Meg!' he said softly.

Her head lifted, her eyes looked into his and her tail beat against the basket. She was all right; she wouldn't suffer too much. It might have ended very differently. Nell was yawning.

'Go back to bed,' Charles said. 'No need for us both to

suffer. I'll try and have a kip later. Maybe Kate and Rob will do a day's work for a change.'

Nell laughed.

'That'll be the day,' she said. She hesitated in the doorway. But now wasn't the time to talk. The idea would have to go on simmering for a day or two longer. She'd better get some rest or she'd be useless too. She pushed her hair out of her eyes, stifled a yawn and went gratefully back to her bed.

Outside the stars died as Charles started the milking and brooded over his phone call to George Merry.

## CHAPTER TWO

▶◆◆◆◆◆◆◀

Nell couldn't sleep. She dressed and went down to the kitchen again, to poke the fire until the wood burned brightly; to mix another bowl of gruel for Meg and examine the bitch carefully. The vet would need to see that bite on her leg, but otherwise she should heal quickly. She would be lame for some days. It was time they had another dog. Nell dreaded the advent of a new pup; the puddles on the floor if she were busy; the need to watch nonstop to prevent damage; to teach the baby manners.

Charles hadn't time. Meg had been easy, but new pups varied and she would be tied for a while to the feeding routine. None of the men could cope with a baby needing four meals a day and constant attention till it was old enough to know the rules of its home.

She wanted to warn Kate that her father had had a bad night, but when Kate ran a bath Nell sighed, knowing it would be useless. There'd be complaints about cold water.

Kate was in love again—an event that so far had happened five times, each time being the great event of her life. She was singing at the top of her voice.

'I could have danced all night.'

Nell only hoped her daughter would come down to earth before the farm woke up and went about its business. Charles, busy milking, was almost asleep on his feet, and anyone annoying him would earn the flash of his tongue and his quick violent temper. It was usually over and done with fast, but at times his brooding anger lay about the house, and nothing would lift it.

She sighed, and scrambled eggs, buttered toast, made tea. Meg watched every movement, basking by the fire, resting. She would have preferred Charles to be there, but the bitch was not feeling well enough to go out and look for him. Her leg hurt, her body ached, and she was unusually reluctant to move. Kate was in her bedroom now, still singing. She had changed the tune to one of the more modern rock songs that Nell hated. The rhythm jarred, and her head ached. She had lain awake for hours, thinking of Charles out in the icy fields, knowing how cold he would be, worrying about him. He wasn't a young man any more. And he hated killing.

He had shot their last dog three years before, when Bruin was trapped by a runaway tractor, lying under the brute of a thing with his back broken. Meg had leaped out of the way. There was no hope, and it would have meant the dog staying there, half dead, for hours before the tractor could be lifted off him. The vet was out on a farm, busy with a calving. Charles had taken his gun.

Once the tractor was safe, he had gone off for the day. She never knew where. The Land Rover had driven out of the yard, and her husband vanished. He came home long after she was asleep and never spoke of Bruin again. If Meg had died . . .

She must start hunting for a new pup. That at least she could do. Tom would know of litters due; know which dog had sired them and the history of the bitch. Charles liked to buy from an older bitch, one that had had at least two previous litters; he liked to know the temperament of her

19

puppies and had to be sure of his stud dog. Tom was retired; he had been a shepherd for them for a very long time and it would give him an interest. Maybe he'd come in and help with the baby days, with the teaching of the little animal . . . he'd been a good man in his time and had trained some good dogs. He'd won many cups at the local Trials.

Kate erupted into the room. Her jeans were too tight for working, the beautiful thick jersey was absurd. Her hair lay soft and thick and dark on her shoulders, newly washed. It was ridiculous to dress like that on the farm, but Rob would be looking at her. Nell swallowed her words and put the plate in front of her daughter.

Kate cut the rind off the bacon and whistled to Meg.

'Let her rest.' Nell took the bacon to the bitch. It was her morning treat. She nosed it, savouring the taste.

'What's up with her?' Kate had her mouth full, one eye on her magazine, the other on her plate.

'She was in a fight last night.'

Kate swallowed, and turned to the agony page which never failed to fascinate her. People had such extraordinary problems.

'Did Dad get the fox?'

'It wasn't a fox. It was George Merry's dog.' And they had to ring George and tell him Sam was lying dead in their sheep field with Charles's bullet in his head. Charles would brood about that all day.

'Oh, lord, I'd better get cracking. Is Dad in much of a state?' She only half listened to the answer, shrugging into her anorak, to go out and feed the baby calves from the bucket. She went across to the milking parlour to fetch the milk.

'So you decided to get up,' Charles said morosely to Betsebel's udder.

'It's not late.' Kate was indignant. She was much earlier than usual. Rob was due on duty soon. Rob, with his dark hair and the laughter in his eyes, and his quick teasing manner. She could think of little else.

Charles grunted. Time to take the cups off Betsebel; time to wash down Daisybel; and Rob ought to have been here by now. He was lodging with old Tom and his wife. Not a mile away, but he still couldn't be early. Blow doing favours for friends, the boy would never make a farmer— all he had eyes for was Kate, who certainly brightened up the place, but distracted the younger men. Not that she intended to. Charles looked out of the door. Darkness had vanished and it was a fresh bright day, frost lying hard on the ground, the sun brilliant in a sky that had forgotten clouds. Somewhere a blackbird sang.

'I want you and Rob to go over and fetch the ram,' Charles said, seeing it in his mind's eye, the beast he had dreamed of for years. The perfect animal; he couldn't fault it, unless the head was a shade over long, the ears a fraction off the ideal position. With his ewes . . . he had plans for his flock. The best in the county.

Kate looked at her father's back. The ram. She knew all about the ram. They had the wretched animal for break-fast, lunch and tea. Should her father buy him? It was a lot of money. And you could say that again, Kate thought irritably, filling both buckets with warm milk, avoiding the cowpats in the farmyard, going into the calf shed to look at her charges. They were waiting, eager for their break-fast. They were pretty things and she stroked the warm noses before each dipped its head to the bucket and drank. She hated the sweet sour smell of the straw they stood on. Another job she loathed was waiting for her—cleaning out the pens.

The ram. If her father had opted for a cheaper animal she could have had her own car. It was ridiculous to be tied here, unable to go anywhere unless her father or her mother or one of the men gave her a lift, and even then she couldn't be certain of a lift back. Unless it were with Rob. He'd be here soon. They would be together all morn-ing, fetching the ram. And then they could go off to the Plough for lunch. They deserved a break. Working here day in, day out, all hours. Her father never thought of her as a human being, just another hand on the farm. Feed the calves and muck them out. Feed the pigs and muck them out. Clean the dairy. Clean the milking parlour, work on the farm as if she were a man not a woman. A vague unease, a thought of women's lib and equal rights crossed her mind, but she was no militant. She enjoyed being a girl; she enjoyed the looks the men cast her; enjoyed knowing she was attractive, and enjoyed her ability to tease her father, most days, into forgiving her for yet another piece of outrageous behaviour. Like taking the day off without asking and leaving him totally without extra help on the day of the big Agricultural Fair. She had been lent a horse for the showjumping and she was going to jump and blow him. She'd come second. The rosette hung in her room. If he wouldn't buy her a car he might at least buy her a horse. She wanted a horse so passionately that she sometimes went down the road to yearn over the fence at the ponies their neighbour bred, and to beg a ride on his mare.

She'd love to have Lottie. She was so pretty; a gay, dancing sprite, light as one of her mother's sponge cakes, lifting over the hurdles and fences as if they weren't there. With a mare like Lottie she could have ridden with the best of them at Olympia. She saw herself dressed like Marian Mold, heard the wild clapping as she completed a clear round and Lottie danced in delight, knowing she'd done well; and then she returned abruptly to reality, cursed as the calf she was feeding moved suddenly, butting the bucket, and milk poured over her legs.

Rob, standing in the doorway, laughed at her.

'Doesn't do to forget to concentrate,' he said, taking the bucket from her. 'Go and change. We're off to fetch his Majesty and bring him to his harem. Your Dad's in a rare old bate after his night out, and George Merry's here, heard about his dog.'

'Oh, Lord.' Kate raced over the cobbles, almost slipping on a patch of ice. She dodged upstairs, but could not avoid hearing George's voice.

'Sorry it was my fellow; I'd have shot him myself if I'd known.' There was no blame in his tone. Only regret.

'I wish you had shot him, and not me,' Charles said. 'I hate doing it to any dog, worse when it's a friend's dog.'

'No hard feelings. I'll take him over to the vet.' Kate could hear the voices through the floor, as she changed, leaving the milk-soaked jeans on her bedroom floor for her mother to find and sigh over when she came upstairs to make the bed.

'I'll pay for a post mortem, and if I was wrong, I'll buy you a new dog,' Charles said.

'He was there with the sheep. Not much more evidence needed, but we'll have the vet look at his inside and see if there's sheep inside him; put your mind at rest.' George knew Charles well. The voices died away as the two men went outside, and Kate, glancing out of the window, saw them walk across the yard towards the far fields where Charles had spent the night.

She liked the sheep. They were Suffolks, children's toy sheep, plushy faces, sturdy bodies, long backs, beautifully curved necks, their bodies white, their heads endearingly black with well-spread ears; their short legs were also black. They were, to her mind, the prettiest of all sheep, but three thousand guineas on a ram was going it steep. Dad could have got a good one easily for six or seven hundred pounds, and upgraded the ewes with that.

His Majesty indeed. They'd have to treat him tenderly, have to watch every second of the day lest anything happen to him. And Mackie, their retiring ram, wouldn't like an upstart around the place one little bit.

Three thousand guineas. What she couldn't do with that money. A car. A horse. Her father's views were so limited. He was getting old and had forgotten what it felt like to be twenty, almost twenty-one; to want to run all day and dance all night; to wear pretty clothes and to have fun. There was no fun here. The highlight of her life had been the village hop a few weeks ago. She had had a new dress that her mother had made for her. Big deal. Anyone would think they were paupers. Everything went back into the bally farm. And now they were having a ram that cost so much it would be a nightmare. Suppose it got ill? Suppose it died? Suppose it wasn't fertile? That would be a laugh.

'Are you ever coming?' Rob shouted up the stairs.

'Coming.' She was flying down toward him, and Nell, emerging from the kitchen, a nagging ache in her side from carrying too heavy a load the day before, was suddenly envious. It wasn't fair. Aging was a penalty no woman should have to endure. They'd been like that once, she and Charles. A century ago.

She watched the race across the cobbles to the waiting Land Rover; the trailer was coupled to it. Drive carefully, she said to herself and to any God who might be listening, knowing Rob. Take care of that ram, he's our future, too much of our future; a stake we can't afford, we shouldn't afford, but who am I to say no to bettering our stock, to letting Charles realise a dream. Only—where are my dreams? She looked out at the morning, at the frost white on the ploughland, at a bird skimming across rimed grass, at the sheep in the fields and the cattle by the gate, waiting to go back to the day's grazing. The men were at work already. The vet was due to see one of the cows. He could look at Meg. She had work to do. Food for the men and the beds to make. And, when she went upstairs, the milk stain from Kate's jeans to get out of the carpet. The idea that had been niggling for days flared into life. She would have to convince Charles. He would argue, but she was sure she was right.

She glanced out of the window. Rob was driving out of the yard. He had forgotten, as ever, to close the gate and the cattle were there. The boy had nothing in his head at all. No one would dream he was a farmer's son. No wonder his father wanted him taught by someone else. He was enough to drive a saint mad, and so was Kate. Youth was something they'd both grow out of, but others suffered while they did the growing. She ran down the stairs and across the yard and closed the gate, and stood to catch her breath.

It was a beautiful morning. There were the first small signs of buds swelling on the branches. Her apple tree would be in blossom in a few short weeks; and there was the hint of a pink glow on the almond, and daffodils massed on the bank behind the house. The cattle stood, heads down, and the sheep were lying cuddled against the ground. It looked so peaceful, an idyllic life—until you saw a sheep move carefully and knew a lamb was due and there might be trouble; and one of the other sheep was carrying a leg high. She'd have to ask Charles if he knew. There'd been too much foot trouble this winter.

Bills for extra feed. Bills for the vet. And now the ram. The thought of the money Charles had paid for him danced in front of her eyes. She would have liked new furniture; she hated the heavy Victorian stuff she had inherited, but it was all good. Too good to throw away. One day she'd get her father's little desk valued. She had always meant to. Her father had said it was worth a considerable sum. It didn't look it. She didn't even like it.

Nor did she like the big overstuffed chairs and settee. Only the kitchen was comfortable, with its wicker chairs and soft cushions and the rug she had made herself the first winter they were married, when Tim was on the way. She wished she saw more of her son. He came home at rare intervals, rang when he remembered, which wasn't often, flew round the country on his job, and the only news she had of him was through his weekly articles in their farming paper. Articles on beasts that made the headlines. Maybe he would write up his father's new ram, and come home to get the facts straight. It would be good to have him around for a little while.

She went out with coffee for the men. Charles was finishing the cows. He was having the usual trouble with Arabellina, who was everything a cow shouldn't be. She stamped on the men's feet, kicked as they passed her and butted the unwary. She was a pretty cow with an innocent face, but wily as they came.

'Moos and kicks and hanks of hair and stinking cow dung everywhere,' Charles said, as he shoved the awkward animal forcibly through the gate into the Willow Field, and took his coffee mug from Nell. He was quoting from a poem that had amused them all in a long ago issue of the farming paper. One of the men had cut it out and it was taped over Arabellina's stall, along with the red rosette she had won two years ago for the best milk yield. Pity she was such a beast of a cow.

'Come and look at the morning,' Nell said.

'A short breather. I might try and get some sleep after

25

Vic's been to look at that cow. And he can look at Meg too. That bite's nasty.'

Time. There never was enough. Time to stand and stare. Time to think. Time to talk. They both rushed from one job to another, meeting briefly, unable to spare more than a few seconds for the basics of life:

'The vet's coming.'

'We need more cattle cake.'

'Load of hay due.'

'I'm going into Mancaster. Do you want anything?'

'Pass the salt.'

'More coffee?'

If only the days were longer.

The idea Nell had been incubating was growing, but when would they be able to settle down and discuss it properly? Charles had already left her to go across the yard and open the gate for Vic's Land Rover.

'Come into money?' he asked teasingly, eyeing the new vehicle. They were old friends. The vet grinned at Nell.

'He's jealous,' he said.

'Wait till you see my new ram. Then you'll be jealous.' Charles was already leading the way to the cow byre. Nell grinned in her turn.

'He'll be sleeping with that new ram, unable to take his eyes off him or leave him alone for a second,' she said.

'I hope he's insured him,' Vic said soberly. 'It's a hell of a big investment.' It was common knowledge in the village. Paid top price for that ram, had old Charles. Must be off his rocker, said the younger men. The older ones said little and were envious. A ram like that . . .

'Papers are on his desk now,' Nell said. 'Better hurry up, Vic. He was up all night.'

'So I heard,' Vic said. 'George brought his dog in. I've the P.M. to do after lunch. I only hope I do find sheep worrying signs—Charles would never forgive himself if he got the wrong dog, and I'll have to tell him. I'll look at its brain too. Sam's always been a nasty-tempered dog. Don't know why George kept him.'

'Meg's hurt,' Nell said. 'There will be coffee when you come in.'

'And scones, I hope,' Vic said. He was enviably lean. Nell had to watch her weight and was always tempted by her own cooking. She would have liked to put on her coat and drive into the hills and walk for miles, but work would not wait and if she didn't sponge Kate's carpet and soak her jeans, both would be ruined.

Working round the house, she felt again that somewhere life was waiting for her. She was marking time. How did that daft piece of rhyming go? There must be more to life, I'll swear, but cows get in my way. And sheep and rams and dogs, and Charles.

Not to mention Kate, she thought as she walked into the bathroom. There was a tide line round the bath; Kate's socks were soaking in the basin, covered in cow muck, and they should have been in a bucket downstairs. The towels were soaked and on the floor, Kate's hair dryer on the window sill, yesterday's discarded clothes on the chair. There was hair blocking the basin and water refused to run away when she took out the plug and the stained socks. They had been new and white; why on earth did the child have to wear those under her jeans when she had old ones that didn't matter?

Kate made more work than Charles and the men and the dogs put together, and, as she helped on the farm, considered herself exempt from helping round the house, or even making her bed.

Or tidying up. It took more than an hour to clean the bath and basin and the bathroom floor, wash out the stained socks and tidy Kate's room, an hour during which Nell's resolve hardened. She heard voices downstairs and remembered she had promised Vic coffee.

'Meg's OK. Nothing that a couple of days' rest won't heal,' Vic Langton said. He was a big man, broad shouldered, his thick hair grey, his brown eyes brilliant under spiky white brows. Meg adored him; she was rarely ill and Vic was part of her farming life rather than someone she went to for treatment. Her tail beat as he examined her.

'Pity I can't stay till the ram comes. Can't wait to see him. He's the centre of the village gossip at the moment,' Vic said. 'A Solomon among rams; a very Emperor, his harem of beauties waiting. Don't get me wrong,' he added, 'they are beauties. If everyone paid as much attention to detail as Charles . . .'

'I sometimes wish he paid as much attention to me as he does to detail,' Nell said, and then blushed as Vic turned to her. His eyebrows shot up, and his mouth twisted in a quick grin.

'You're as bad as Marie—she complains my patients mean more than she does. It's our livelihood, Nell. Men must work. . . .'

'Oh, I know. I didn't mean a thing. It's a lovely day and I'd like to be out on the hills. . . .'

'And you wish you were Kate,' Vic said.

Nell turned and stared at him.

'I never thought of that,' she said.

'It comes to us all. I look at my two strapping sons and wish I could move that fast again, not noticing the ground beneath my feet, running everywhere, chasing tomorrow. All you and I do is regret yesterday.'

'What on earth are you two looking so solemn about?' Charles said, coming into the room, yawning widely. 'Dear heaven, I'm half dead. I must sleep, Nell. Let me know the result of your P.M. on that dog, Vic. Meg OK?'

'She'll do. Not as young as she was either. You need another pup. Or Meg will be retired and you'll have nothing to take over, unless you buy a trained dog.'

'I train my own; I like to know what goes into that first year. I'd have liked to breed my own from Meg. Wonder why she's barren?'

'A born spinster,' Vic said. 'We could try A.I.'

'On a bitch? If she won't take a dog, and she won't, she fights all of them off, then there's something up and I'm not forcing her to have a litter,' Charles said. 'I did that once before with a barren cow, remember? When A.I. had just started. And got a monster for my pains—a calf with two heads. Funny things happen sometimes.'

'The funniest thing that will happen today is that you won't get any lunch and Vic will never make his afternoon round,' Nell said. 'Look at that clock.'

'Time to go.' Vic went out whistling, picking up another

of Nell's richly buttered scones as he went. Charles stumped wearily upstairs to lie down for an hour, trying to catch up on the sleep that he craved. Nell counted heads. Three men and she and Charles and Kate and Rob. Food for seven. She began to peel potatoes and carrots, to mince the meat for a giant pasty, to put on the mixer and make more scones and a cut-and-come-again cake, full of cherries, that Charles liked so much.

She glanced at the clock. It haunted her, its hands racing round much too fast. They should soon be back with the ram. She looked out of the window at her old car and sighed. It was for ever needing attention. She would have loved a new one; but rams came first and cattle came first and feed came first, and her needs came a long way down the list.

The clock ticked and Meg slept by the fire and the wood crackled. One of the farm cats stalked a bird and missed its prey and sat to wash its paw. It had kittens in the hay, tucked safe and deep in the barn. More ratters, which was just as well. Rob had found a rat nest only the day before with five young in it and destroyed it. Time to collect the eggs; she needed them for the cake and she had forgotten them. Kate should have done them before she went, but Kate's mind was never on her work these days.

If only there were more time for herself; time to sit and do nothing; time to go window shopping; time and money to buy new clothes; to find herself a hobby—she had dedicated herself to her family. She had been Mummy for twenty-four years, nonstop, since Tim was born. She was still Mummy to Kate, who took no responsibility at all. Time Kate grew up. Time she talked to Charles. Time to find time and make decisions. The egg she was holding dropped to the floor and broke. She went to fetch a cloth but when she came back Meg had climbed out of her basket and limped over the floor and was lapping happily at her unexpected bonus. She loved raw eggs, though she would carry one round the farmyard without breaking the shell and Charles often asked her to perform this absurd party trick.

The clock ticked relentlessly and Nell wiped the floor

and went back to the cooker. A vague worry about Rob and Kate nagged at her. Suppose they had an accident with that ram?

Charles would be heartbroken. He had watched it grow; had had his eye on it for over a year, but its owner had not wanted to sell at the price Charles set. It had gone to auction. Nell remembered the bidding vividly, unbelievingly, as the price soared and one man after another dropped out.

'Your man's crazy, missus,' old Harry Compton had said, as he passed her, and thinking of all that they needed on the farm, knowing the state of the bank balance only too well as she did the farm accounts, she agreed, though she smiled and said nothing, leaving Harry wondering if Charles were much warmer than any of them imagined. It was a good farm. But it wasn't that good.

Just as well Harry couldn't see those bank statements, Nell thought.

She paused to watch two bullfinches on the apple tree, their breasts bright in the sun. How lovely to be a bird and fly free.

No ties. No responsibilities, and no Kate to disorder her life so much.

Seven to feed and the work to be done and no end to it.

She sighed and began to set the kitchen table.

If only she had help.

'Meg, I wish you had hands. You're such a willing thing,' she said to the dog, who wagged an enthusiastic tail, not understanding a word but delighted to be noticed. 'I wish I could lie by the fire and bask,' Nell said, and laughed at herself standing there talking to the bitch as if she were human, and realising suddenly that Meg was the only creature round the place that ever had time to listen to her. It was a remarkably sobering thought.

# CHAPTER THREE

◖◆◆◆◆◆◆◆◖

At Marlings, five miles away and down the lane, Joe Makin dressed in his best clothes: a blue suit that hung loosely on him, reminding him that he was not the man he had been; a carefully knotted tie, a beautifully laundered white shirt. He was small and sturdily built, although he had lost some weight. His face was reddened by weather, his eyes unexpectedly vivid blue and penetrating as he looked at his hearers.

He looked round the yard. Everything was perfect; the cobbles were clean, and the stable too. The January Queen grazed in her field and came to him for her morning titbit. He had forgotten it, in his anxiety. She whinnied as he went indoors.

She was a black Shire mare, his winning beauty and almost a champion, though she'd never be a champion now. He hadn't the money to show her, nor the energy to drive to the shows. Eighty years old yesterday and he had to admit it. Still, she had one Championship Certificate to prove her worth. It was pinned on the wall of her stable above the manger with her prize rosettes. He'd farmed here for sixty years; had made the place grow. Worry needled him. Would they let him stay? He had repaired the lower field fence, but the ditch was in need of clearing and he hadn't been able to grass the big field yet; his crops had been low last year and he knew they were badly harvested; he had been late booking the combine and they had come to him last after gales had flattened the barley. They didn't care so long as it was harvested. In former years he would have hand-scythed the flattened corners.

He had had to sell his milking herd. He couldn't get help. No one wanted work on a farm and in any case the wages now were too high. He didn't make that much profit himself. They didn't give a man a chance, what with taxes and levies and not being able to sack a hand if he were useless, as a lot of them were. And the cost of living went up yearly. The men were pricing themselves out of work.

He had struggled alone since Mary died.

If only the farm were his, but he was the tenant. And even sixty years of tenancy didn't give you any rights if it was proved that you couldn't go on. If he fooled them this year, he wouldn't be able to next year.

If only My Lady hadn't sold the farm, but she couldn't live on her money either—rates, taxes and death duties had eaten into her estate and she had come to him unhappily only six months ago to tell him she had to sell.

'I can't go on, Joe,' she had said. 'I'm an old woman. They've beaten me.'

He knew who 'They' were. She and he had joked in a cynical way about 'Them' for years—the governments who never understood the ways of the landed folk or the farmers. They had scythed the motorway through her estate; had taken land from her; had taken vast sums of money from her when her father died. She had to live too. He liked and respected her and they got on well. No side, even if she was My Lady.

They had sat together in his kitchen, sharing unhappiness. He was a good baker and he'd made a batch of scones.

'How's the Queen?'

'I'm going to mate her,' he'd said. 'I haven't chosen the stallion yet.'

'My cousin has a beauty; he'd match the Queen's lines; you'd get a good foal from him. I'll have a word. No stud fee—Joe, I feel so bad about selling this place.'

She'd had a word and now the Queen was in foal. And now the new owners were coming to look over his land;

only two hundred acres, a small place, and it had been in excellent shape until this last year. Bad weather and bad luck had defeated him, but he'd get it back in order this year. All of it. He'd worked till daylight failed, going to bed exhausted, and it showed in his face and his walk.

My Lady had told him they were coming. She had sold to a syndicate, not being able to find private buyer. Men who bought farms and ran them as businesses, turning the animals into cold profits, not understanding that the Queen was a part of his life, not an asset to be sold. She at least was his property. They had no part in her.

He took her bread roll out to her. She adored brown bread and rubbed her nose against his shoulder as he gave it to her.

'That's my beauty,' he said. He rubbed a hand over her, lingeringly, loving the feel of her soft neck. She was his consolation and his pride. If only he could have shown her again; could have gone on judging the horses that were the reason for his existence. He had never wanted anything else. They had made him big money in the old days, before the war.

He turned to face the gate as the Daimler drove in. A uniformed driver, poker faced, and three men in business suits, one of them carrying a neat briefcase. One wore an emerald ring. They got out, looking carefully at the ground before setting highly polished shoes on the cobbles.

One was large, a fat man with small eyes, with several chins and a mean expression. He reminded Joe of a Tamworth pig he had once had, a swine of a boar that never lost a chance to try and nip you when you went near him.

The second was small and dapper, grey haired, grey eyed, grey faced. A man with worries and an ulcer. A man who would never allow a speck of dust to go unnoticed, or a balance sheet unread; who would read the small print and add smaller. A sharp man, a shrewd man, a man to fear.

The third was more like a farmer in an American film; big and polished and suave, dressed in breeches and hacking jacket, a careful pose; a bluff, hearty hail-fellow-well-met manner hiding the best business sense of the three. Joe looked at the cold blue eyes and read beneath the exterior. He had always been clever at summing up a man.

He greeted them quietly. At least dignity was left to him.

He was even older than they had expected and they exchanged glances as he led the way indoors to the big parlour, brightly curtained and cushioned, spotlessly clean, the family pictures on the mantelshelf. A log fire burned in the vast old-fashioned grate. There was a silver tray, a percolator with coffee bubbling, and scones on a silver dish, polished until it shone. Mary's treasured fine china tea service—Joe had been very busy.

They couldn't fool him over prices. He still knew those, even the going rate for lambs and cattle, though he had none. He knew the price of barley. He'd have a good crop come Autumn. The house was in good order, but the man with the ulcer found a broken window cord that Joe had not noticed, a door that would not latch properly, and a patch of dry rot under the porch shelf that he had put up for Mary's plants, more than forty years ago. Where had all that time gone? The thought transfixed him, so that he missed a question. Again eyes met, and this time he saw them, and a cold shiver went through him.

'Is your son likely to come home and help you?' the man had asked.

He had two sons. Both had their own lives and their own families; both lived abroad. Joe was not used to lying, not even white lies.

'I don't know,' he said, knowing perfectly well neither would come back to England. They had much better lives in their new homes. They wrote; and he wondered at the freedom they had, to go fishing, or camping, or visit friends. Life was good over there, they would never come back.

The catechism ended at last and then came the part he had been dreading: the slow patrol of the farm, and the note-taking. He hadn't been aware that the fence in the Ten Acre Pasture was rotten. The piggy man pushed a post and it came away at ground level. So did the next one. And the next.

The Queen never pushed at fences. He hadn't known they were loose.

The stable door had a rusted hinge. He knew that, but it was too heavy for him to hold alone and he had been waiting for My Lady's chauffeur to come and help repair it. Bob had promised, but My Lady kept Bob busy. He was her man of all work, in the grounds and the house, cleaning her guns and training her dogs; eight labradors she had, which she bred and showed, winning prizes with them all the time. Not much longer. Arthritis was claiming her now and she often had to walk with a stick, railing at her infirmity, hating it. She was short-staffed too.

He had missed another question. The walk round the farm became a formality. He took them indoors again, offering them homemade beer. The big bluff man accepted. The thin man asked for a glass of milk and then asked if it were pasteurised. It was. He had to buy his own milk now. He hadn't even one cow to provide for him. The piggy man stood at the window, twirling a small gold coin that he wore on a watch chain. It reminded Joe of his grandfather's watch chain. The old man's watch was upstairs but it had stopped going ten years before, died of old age, the watchmaker said. He could have new works but they cost too much.

'I'm sorry,' the bluff man said, spokesman for the three, 'but it is time you had a rest, Mr. Makin. Eighty's a good age, and I think this farm needs a younger man to run it.'

Joe nodded. He couldn't argue. He hadn't hoped for anything else, except as a daydream that he knew to be a fairy tale.

'My Lady knows of a good Home for you, where her housekeeper and her own retired cowman are living,' the small man said, sipping his milk, refusing to look at Joe, aware that they were giving him a life sentence, not that the old man had much life left. Ridiculous trying to run this place on his own. Ridiculous to feel pity. The mare ought to fetch a good price. The old boy would have to pay dilapidations when he left; no use being soft-hearted in this game—it was the law. About a thousand pounds in all the old boy would have to find, at a rough estimate. He'd have money salted away. They always did.

Joe knew the Home. It was good, as homes went, and he had visited Mrs. Lewis there. She had her own room and her own things about her, but she wished there wasn't so much routine: in bed by ten like children, no TV after 9.30 and pap to eat as if your stomach had packed up for ever. Mrs. Lewis liked a nice bit of Dundee cake but he had to smuggle it in to her. They'd chuckled together like schoolchildren over it. The Home provided sponge cakes.

He'd never liked Sid the cowman. Be a penance to be cooped up with him day after day and the place hadn't big grounds; a little garden and a pool to sit by. Nowhere for horses. His face whitened. He hadn't thought about the Queen. He'd have to sell her.

'Can you be out in six weeks? There's a local auction on the first of the month, you can put the mare in that. She's yours, isn't she, not part of the farm? And then there'll be nothing to keep you. I'll ask My Lady to make arrangements.'

They were gone, the car driving down the lane, leaving a plume of smoke behind it, an insult on the clean air. Treating him as if he were senile, a parcel to be dumped, a nuisance to be removed. He could not swallow the scone he had taken from the plate. He went outside and gave it to the Queen and stood beside her for a long time, watching the sky change from blue to grey, darkening as his world had darkened.

It began to rain.

He led the Queen to her stable and sat beside her on the stool, as he had so many times before, beside so many cows and so many mares, and memory came to plague him.

He went indoors at last. His shotgun stood in the corner of the little sitting room he used at night. He looked at it for a long time. But that was coward's way out and he wasn't taking it. Death would come in its own time—not so long now. The world seemed a little remote, but the Queen was not remote. He could not bear the thought of her being sold. He went to sleep at last, a sleep that was like a small dying: dreamless, exhausted, beyond despair.

Morning came. The weeks went by. There were chores to do and the Queen to be tended, and he had to carry on even though his time with her was so short. A letter came from the Home—My Lady had arranged for him to live there. There were details to be sorted, and he did not want to sort them. He'd have little enough to live on. The State would have to care for him now.

A letter arrived from the auctioneers. The men who called on him had arranged for the mare to be sold, to be collected. The date was there, in writing. It danced in his mind. He could not bear to part with her, but he had to part. He could not bear to tend her, but she had to be tended. They were knifing him, killing him by slow inches, dreadfully. My Lady did not visit or phone. She couldn't face him.

The days fled by, although he willed time to stand still, willed himself to wake and find nightmare had caught him. He stood by the Queen for endless hours, his eyes hungry, knowing she was better than anything he had ever bred before, that the foal would be a champion, even if it was never shown. He had wanted a filly foal, another brood mare. Seven more months before it was born. In someone else's stable. How did you survive total misery? He left the broken fence posts; the ditch was another man's problem now; someone else would prune his roses—would maybe rip them up and plant other flowers. Death was preferable to this, but he couldn't die.

# CHAPTER FOUR

◆◆◆◆◆◆◆◆◀

Rob whistled as he drove. The Land Rover was old and slow, but he had Kate beside him and they could take the whole morning. He didn't want to farm but his father had insisted he try. He envied Tim who'd got away. If it hadn't been for Kate, Rob wouldn't have stayed. For Kate he might even become a farmer. The sun was shining and all the day was theirs.

'We'll have lunch at the Plough,' he said. 'Time on our own, away from everyone. I can't look at you with everyone else there.'

Kate grinned to herself. She was content to just sit and be driven, anywhere in the world so long as Rob was the driver. He was fun to be with, with a quick sense of the ridiculous that stood him in good stead, as when he made a major mistake he could usually take his employer's mind off it by clowning, so that the men laughed. It was hard for Charles to be angry when no one else was annoyed.

One day Rob might marry Kate; they'd be rich and he'd fill her fields with horses. He didn't much care whether they had horses or not, but Kate did. And then maybe they wouldn't marry. Life lay ahead and there were other girls. He didn't want to settle down and think of responsibilities for a long time yet. He was only twenty. He whistled as he drove and Kate joined him, singing the words to his tunes.

They were free—away from the farm and the cattle and the constant feeding and cleaning, the squawk of hens; dodging the scurrying cock and the wicked gander. Rob loathed the gander with a deep undying hatred. The huge bird guarded the place; he guarded the geese and he had never accepted Rob, who was the last comer, an interloper, not belonging in the bird's eyes. 'Diabolo', Kate had christened him and he deserved the name. He claimed all the territory around the duck pond as his own, and the orchard as well. Charles liked having him there; there wasn't a child in the village who'd dare scrump apples with Diabolo around.

Rob always had to make sure the gander wasn't in sight. Diabolo raced down the yard, wings wide, hissing horribly, a mass of indignation. 'Get off my land. Go away. I hate you. You don't belong.' His cackles were almost understandable. It never failed to make the other men laugh and even Kate had to laugh at times, as Rob dived into a barn or the cowshed, slamming the door behind him, leaving the gander hissing and angry, to settle his wings and waddle back to his consorts.

Meg, when she was a puppy, had tried to herd the geese. Diabolo soon taught her that that was unwise, and now dog and gander had a wary relationship, tolerating one another, but never intruding on one another's territory.

Even though Rob drove the longest way round he could think of, they came all too soon to Torrance's farm. Amby Torrance was a bore. Both Rob and Kate were agreed on that, but they had to endure him. They had to get the ram. They would not get away easily. Rob eyed the fields as he climbed out of the Land Rover. The old man had a fortune in sheep there. Hundreds of sheep. It was insane to tie up your money like that. His father did the same thing with pedigree shorthorns. Jack Leicester had just paid a fortune for a bull. Mad as Kate's dad, though the bull was astronomical in price compared with the ram. Hundreds of thousands of pounds as against a few thousand.

People!

If he had all that money he'd fly with Kate to a tropical island and they'd wine and dine and dance all night; soft lapping seas and sandy beaches and palm trees. A plush hotel and splendid food. Rob loved food and the first unkind contours of good living were beginning to show. He had to watch his weight too. He did more than justice to Nell's cooking.

Amby had heard the Land Rover and was waiting for them. He was an enthusiast. He talked sheep, dreamed of sheep, worked with his sheep, smelled like a sheep. He had a good shepherd but drove the man mad because he hated others doing his work. He loved shearing, loved working with his animals, enjoyed lambing time, watching the lambs as they were born, feeding those whose dams had little enough milk, coming out daily to look at them, to brood over them, to note them as they grew. Were they worthy of his flock? Was that ewe worth keeping? His rams were sought after; they were fine upstanding beasts, even the poorest of them, and the best, the one that even Charles was unable to buy, made other men's eyes gleam with envy when they saw him.

No doubt about it, Amby had a unique touch when it came to breeding sheep: an instinctive knowledge, born in him, and fostered in him by both his father and his grandfather. He had stood at the old man's side, when only two years old, learning the finer points of the rams and ewes; had had a good ewe every year as his birthday present from his grandfather and when the old man died had inherited his flock. Added to his father's flock, added to his father's knowledge . . . they'd been sought after as judges and Amby still was. Show under Amby and win a prize and you knew you'd a good beast. He was a very hard judge.

Enthusiasm mastered him now, as always.

'Come and see Monarch,' he said, positive nothing would please Rob and Kate more. 'He's in a show in about nine weeks' time. A sponsored show with good prize money for once. Not enough people sponsor the farming shows. It costs money to enter. £6 for a pen and five days there—costs time. There ought to be a better reward for your trouble.' He threw open the gate of the yard and whistled.

The ram that came trotting out was a Wiltshire, a fine beast with the splendid curved horns that were treasured by crook makers; they made wonderful carved heads. It came to Amby who rubbed it under its chin and gave it a piece of bread from his pocket.

'Call him Trot, Monarch's a mouthful,' Amby said, his eyes eating the ram. He was a tiny, sprightly man with a jaunty walk, his white hair beautifully cut, curling on his head, always immaculate in jodhpurs and a hacking jacket, though as far as Rob knew he had never even sat on a horse's back. His boots reflected the sun.

Amby turned his head, looking contentedly over fields rising to the horizon, thick with sheep.

'I'm crossing the Wiltshires on my Welsh ewes,' he said. 'It's a useful cross, makes good beasts. Some of mine topped sixty guineas apiece at the last sales.' A magpie flew over, a trail of straw in its beak.

'They're nesting in the elm, and that's dying—I'll have to have it down as soon as I can. Pesky beasts, but they're showy birds for all that. One for sorrow. Well, there's always sorrow. Wouldn't be alive if there weren't. No one can be happy for ever and wouldn't appreciate it if they were.'

Oh, shut up and get on with it, Kate thought, as she made appropriate noises about the ram.

'Your Dad get that killer dog yet?' Amby asked. 'It's my turn tonight if he didn't . . . don't suppose he did.'

'He did,' Kate said. 'Meg fought it. She's going to be laid up for a few days. She had a bad bite on her leg.'

'Tell your Dad he can borrow my Glen till she's better. I've three dogs and my new young one's doing a treat. Glenny'll do him fine; works for anyone and well trained. Brings in his sheep as easy as throwing away sixpence.'

'I'll tell him,' Rob said. 'He wants the ram at the double.' He hoped it would stop the old man talking. He wanted to be alone with Kate.

'Can't hurry with beasts. It never does. Ram's in shed near the house all ready for you, but wife's been baking and says come and sample her scones. Kate always liked them as a little lass. I remember when you were no higher than my knee; you ate like a little wolf though, fine cub

41

you were. It's a long time ago now. Annie said she'd like to see you.'

The time was creeping by. Amby had never been known to hurry and she couldn't offend Annie. Her mother would kill her if she did. She and Annie had been at school together and still met whenever possible to talk over old times and also, probably, to grumble about their children. Annie had a son and a daughter as well. Rita was studying music in college and Donald was in Agricultural College like a nice dutiful son.

They followed Amby into the big farm kitchen. There were settles round the wall, a bright rug on the floor, a huge table, scrubbed to whiteness. Annie had inherited it from her mother and it was too useful to replace. It was covered now with a clean linen cloth, and plates of scones and cakes and cups of coffee stood waiting. The smell of baking pervaded the room, so that Rob found himself hungry, just looking, and as he had had no breakfast, he was glad to sit drinking the hot excellent brew, and feast on scones thickly spread with homemade butter, with strawberry jam and with dollops of cream. Annie had been born in Cornwall. They knew how to feed you down there. He grinned at Kate, food quelling his impatience.

The room was papered in white and hung with hunting scenes. There was a new picture over the mantelpiece—a racehorse, elegant, regal, beautiful.

'That's a beauty,' Kate said, eyeing it. That would be a horse to own; long legs for running, a deep chest with room for large lungs for deep breathing, and a heart in him that would outlast every other beast in the field. And a beauty to look at—gleaming with health, head held high, neck arched, the mane and tail flowing as if the horse were running along the wind.

'My brother painted it for me,' Amby said. 'It's in training in Brighton. Won two races and coming on nicely, and siring one or two that show promise. I always wanted to breed horses like your grandad, but I never got the chance. Chance is a wonderful thing, and without it no one makes good. Take your luck and make your luck, is what I say. And if the cards don't fall the way you want them, then make the best of the hand you've got. But never sit back and let things happen to you; that doesn't work at all. I couldn't breed racehorses, so I bred rams instead. Had a few champions in my time.'

Rob ate a fifth scone and drained his coffee cup. Kate's fingers were beating an impatient tattoo on her knee.

'Come and get the ram,' Amby said, 'and drive as if you've got the Crown Jewels aboard, lad. Three thousand pounds and more I got for him; the cheque cleared yesterday.'

Kate made a face at Rob behind Amby's back. The whole world knew how much Charles had paid. The old man was leading the way across the yard.

He opened the door of one of the pens, and the ram came out, head down, butting at Rob, who was standing too near.

Rob jumped out of the way and Amby laughed and whistled to his dog, which was lying, eager, ears pricked, waiting to be told to get on with his job.

'If that ram were a dog, I'd shoot it; it's got a swine of a temper,' Amby said, grinning at Rob, amused by his antics. Kate was watching him exaggerate his movements, clowning as he always did. She laughed. 'As it is, Kate, he'll do your dad proud. Breed him some fine sheep. Those Suffolk ewes of his are little beauties and they breed well. Healthy flock your dad always has.'

He flicked a finger as Rob opened the trailer door and lowered the ramp. The dog was behind the ram, chivvying him, sending him towards the trailer. Amby had called in a second dog, and they worked together, needing no commands.

The ram turned on the first dog and the second ran in, barking, so that he turned again. There was a dog on either side of him and the ram lowered his head and stared at them, but they watched, bodies crouched, and one suddenly flew forward. The ram was into the trailer whether he liked it or not and Amby shut the door.

Kate looked at the animal; at his thick coat, creamy plush against his black legs, at his black head, and neat ears. She had to admit he was a handsome beast. But over

43

three thousand pounds . . . for a beast that would turn into meat in the end, even if it were only dog meat.

'He's all muscle and strong as a horse,' Amby said. He gave the ram one last yearning look. 'I didn't want to sell him, but I've two more even better in my pens. An old fellow and a young one, and no one can buy those, not for double the price of this one. They're for my ewes. Breed me a ram better than this fellow, I shouldn't wonder.'

The old boy was always rambling on; getting senile—he must be over sixty, Rob thought, knowing a man was well over the hill by thirty. He'd be over the hill himself in another ten years and never lived at all. He'd have to do something about that.

The ram thumped an angry hoof against the trailer door every time the Land Rover stopped for a turning or for traffic lights. Bad-tempered as old Mackie, Kate thought and better make sure they don't meet. The thought of the money rankled. If she had all that money she wouldn't be spending it on sheep.

They drew up in the yard.

Two hooves slammed against the door.

'He's a devil,' Kate said. 'Let's get him out and get to the Plough. I'm sick of being a farmer's daughter. It's a gorgeous afternoon. We could go for a drive; no one will miss us, as long as we're back for milking.'

'Thou, Eve, tempted me,' Rob said. 'Comfort me with apples and kiss me like a King's Consort. We'll be in trouble when we get home though.'

'We always are in trouble.' Kate said, as the hooves beat against the door again. She was tired of working. Other people had days off; she'd pinch a day off and take Rob with her. They'd never be able to have this day again. They hardly ever saw one another. A brief meeting behind the barn, a visit to the pub in the evening, but she always had jobs to do and so had he.

'Let's get him out,' Rob said. There was no one about and he gave Kate a quick kiss. 'We'll have that day off. Steal it out of time, live now and pay later.'

She laughed up at him, all thought of anything but an afternoon out driven out of her head. He gripped her hand

44

and they stood, unaware of anything but each other. An afternoon together seemed so little to ask.

She opened the field gate and Rob backed the Land Rover. No fear of the ram getting free. Kate shut the gate again, and Rob went to the back of the trailer and opened it, letting down the ramp.

Time was racing past and the wretched animal wouldn't come out. There was no sign of Mackie. Her father would have put him in one of the byres. The gate at the top of the field was open but that only led to a second field, where the ram often grazed. No sign of him there either.

'All safe,' Kate said, wanting to get the ram out quickly and go off with Rob.

The new ram came out of the van, stamping. Kate shooed him to the end of the field, where he stood, head down, glowering. Just time to get the Land Rover backed into the yard again. She stood by the gate, taking care not to leave a gap through which the ram could come charging back to gain his freedom. He wouldn't like being in a new place. Animals were very conservative. He stood, head up, sniffing the air, uncertain and Kate, looking at him, was forced to admit that he was the most magnificent beast she had ever seen in her life. No wonder her father had been tempted; if she had the chance of a horse of that quality she'd mortgage her soul and maybe even give Rob up too. She turned to go out of the gate.

Somewhere behind her she heard an outraged noise that she couldn't identify. It was like no noise she had ever heard in her life before. Mackie was at the far end of the field, almost through the far gate, hundreds of feet away from her, running at full pelt, head lowered, emitting this astonishing noise.

'Rob!'

There was panic in her voice.

It was too late to do a thing. Mackie had been lying in a hollow, out of the wind. He heard the newcomer and he moved, faster than he had ever moved in his life, challenging the intruder.

He roared in anger. Another ram in his field. On his territory. Near his ewes.

Anger gave him a power that had been missing for almost a year.

The two rams met head on, at full gallop, as the newcomer turned to challenge.

There was a long squeal as Mackie shouted his triumph.

The new ram lay dead on the ground, his neck broken, caught by the savage thrust between his ears, totally off balance. Kate stood white-faced. Rob's hands were shaking.

Kate felt sick. She was not sure that she wouldn't be sick.

She ought to have looked in the far field. She ought to have checked. She knew what happened when a new animal was brought to the farm. It was a long-standing rule that they were never introduced to the other beasts till they had settled in; that any introduction was done with the greatest of care, with every precaution taken.

Nell came running out of the house. She raced down the field.The ram's head was lolling. His neck was broken. She was so angry and miserable she dared not speak. Kate couldn't speak. Rob was leaning on the gate, as if his legs were going to give way any moment.

Nell stood up. Charles had dreamed of that ram for months; had brooded over him as he grew; had saved and saved and mortgaged the year's profit for him; and the insurance wasn't yet paid. The form was on the desk, the cheque newly written. She didn't know what to say or do.

'Who's going to tell your father?' she asked Kate.

Kate ran.

Rob followed her.

'For God's sake let's get out of here. I'll face Dad after lunch. I can't face him now.'

'We must,' Rob said. 'It won't be any better for waiting.'

'If you don't take me away from here I'll never speak to you again.' Kate couldn't think. Panic overwhelmed her, and she couldn't face her father's eyes; her mother's had been bad enough. Nell was still standing beside the dead

46

ram, as if wishing and praying and willing would bring him back to life. As if it would save Charles from the discovery. Perhaps Amby would sell them another, but they hadn't the money. This was a dead loss. A total loss. A loss they couldn't afford.

Kate and Rob were still arguing. The three farm hands had come and joined Nell.

No one could have failed to hear the din. Surely Charles had heard too.

'Dear God,' Bert said. 'Hey, missus, you look terrible. Go on in and get yourself a drink of sherry or something; I'll tidy up here. Is Kate going to tell the Gaffer?'

'I hope so,' Nell said bleakly. 'I can't. Can you? Can any of us? Bert, it isn't even insured.'

They turned as Rob drove out of the yard, tyres screaming. Kate had run away. Nell had thought better of her daughter than that and was deeply disappointed.

Mackie, his enemy defeated, was grazing quietly. He was due to be retired; they would have to use one of his sons, but not one of the four young rams were a patch on this. She had never seen anything so magnificent in her life. Even in death it was a glorious animal.

'It will butcher,' Bert said, meaning to be consoling, but it was no consolation at all and Nell turned and walked quickly into the farmhouse, and stood by Meg, wishing she could sit by the bitch and cuddle her close and cry hot tears of misery into her fur. Meg, aware of human suffering, licked Nell's hand.

Charles came down the stairs.

'Lunch ready?' he asked.

He glanced at Nell.

'What in heaven's the matter?'

'Better come here, Boss,' Bert said, his tone ominous. Charles glanced at his wife and walked out into the yard. Nell could not be bothered to dish up the lunch. She waited for an explosion but there was total silence from outside. Not a man spoke. A cow lowed somewhere in the field. Charles passed by the window. She could not see his face.

A moment later she heard the Land Rover engine start.

Charles drove out of the yard. Two of the men came by, carrying the dead ram. Bert came indoors.

'I'll get dinner on the table,' Nell said. Her face felt wooden.

'Gaffer won't be back till late, I reckon,' Bert said. 'Took it hard.'

Nell, cutting a giant piece of pie, adding carrots and potatoes and gravy, handed the plate to Bert. 'What did he say?'

'Not a word. Bent down and looked and looked, and lifted the poor devil up. Then he turned and went off. Reckon there'll only be four of us for lunch.'

Nell gave a half smile. Bert had been with them for years. He was an untidy giant of a man, red-haired and red-faced with huge hands that were astonishingly gentle with an injured beast. He was doing his best to ease the moment, to gloss over the trouble, to offer comfort without knowing how, and she was grateful.

The other two men came in. They sat and ate, talking in monosyllables about the jobs needing doing that afternoon.

Nell, brooding over the dishes, went out into the byre, where Bert was busy with the calves. Kate's job and she wasn't there to do it.

'Bert, do you know how it happened?'

'Canoodling, I reckon,' Bert said unhappily. 'Kate and Rob, they've no time for anything but each other. Give them a moment off and they're kissing behind the cowshed; they were in a hurry and only thinking of each other. Not my place to say so, but as long as young Rob's here, we'll have problems. Kate's not doing her share, and neither is he. He's a nice enough lad, but it's a chancy set up.'

She should have seen it coming. Rob would have to go and she would have to make Charles listen to her. It was high time to put her plan into action. She began to clean the kitchen for the second time that day, anxious to keep her hands busy and her mind occupied, not wanting to think ahead to the evening when Charles came back and Kate came home.

'Oh Meg, Meg,' she said.

The bitch wagged her tail, and sought her water bowl. The kitchen was filled with the sound of her quick lapping. Thank heaven for the dog, Nell thought. Company and sympathy and unable to talk at all. No questions asked and none to answer.

The telephone rang. How much hay was Charles wanting? He'd rung the night before. Nell wrote the caller's name and phone number down on the pad. Life had to go on. All afternoon her mind was occupied with the vision of the dead ram, and of the cheque for the insurance. She found the form and read it. No let out there.

She willed the clock to stop, and time to stand still.

Then, as the hurrying minutes passed and neither her husband nor her daughter returned, she began to worry. What would Charles do? Where would he go? Suppose he drove too fast and had an accident? Suppose Kate and Rob eloped. She had visions of them driving to Gretna Green, of a policeman coming to tell her her husband was dead, killed in a crash, and when a vehicle drove into the yard she dared not look out of the window.

It was only Ned knacker come for the carcase of the ram.

'A bad business, missus,' he said, over the tea and scones she could not refuse to offer.

It wasn't much of an epitaph for the most expensive ram in the whole of the farm's history.

# CHAPTER FIVE
◆◆◆◆◆◆◆◆◀

Charles took the road to the hills. There was peace up there, almost in the clouds. The world below him was remote; he was no longer part of it. He looked down, on valleys and farms, on fields and hedges and moving sheep. He could find another ram, though it would take years to find one as good. Nobody bred that quality every day. Quality. It was a passion with him; and with Amby. He would have to tell Amby, who at least had been paid . . . but it wasn't only the money.

Charles had watched the ram grow, had watched it develop into the kind of beast men turned into a legend. Like Sirrah, the sheepdog that was in the ancestry of so many good dogs. He turned his thoughts to a new pup. Meg was four; she was now their only dog, since Bruin died. And that had been a brutal business too.

Thought was bad company even here. It would be a long time before he could forget. A long time before he could forgive his daughter. Most of all it was impossible to forgive her for running off, for not telling him, herself, what had happened. It had been a long time before he got the facts from the men.

Nell would be worrying. Charles sighed and turned for home. He drove slowly, reluctant to face Kate, afraid of what he might say. He hoped Ned had collected the ram. He didn't want any reminders of one of the worst day's work he remembered. Kate knew the hazards; that was what he couldn't forgive. Why hadn't she checked the field to see where Mackie was?

50

And then he remembered that on any other day he would have taken Mackie from the field himself. He had gone to bed, exhausted after being up all night. Kate had relied on him to do his share of the job. He was as much to blame. She was very young. It didn't make him feel any better, and he had a nagging headache and a need for food when at last he drove into the yard.

Everywhere was quiet. The men had stayed late and there wasn't a hand's turn of work left for him to do. The yard was hosed and swept and clean; the cattle in the sheds, and two new lambs side by side in the little barn they called the orphanage. They looked at him with sleepy eyes. The clean empty bottles stood side by side on the shelf, and he took them to fill again for the late night feed.

The kitchen was bright and warm, Nell sitting in the big armchair, glancing at a magazine. She couldn't settle at all. Kate wasn't home. Meg climbed out of her basket and ran to greet her master, her sleek body wagging all over, her head and her tail almost meeting, squealing with pleasure, carrying her lame leg, but obviously well on the mend. Charles petted her, and sat by the fire, grateful to Nell for saying nothing.

'Food?' she asked.

His fingers found the warm place on Meg's chest that sent her crazy with delight when it was scratched. She sat, a besotted expression in her eyes, head up, ears flat, enjoying the caress.

Charles nodded. His brief rest had done no good at all. His body ached with its need for sleep, but he would have to eat. He watched Nell lay the table. She had waited for him. She set two places only. So Kate was still out. His mouth tightened and Nell guessed his thoughts. This wasn't the time for speaking. He needed food and a rest, and if they spoke during the meal it would be safe of trivialities.

'Message about some hay,' she said, remembering, as she put a steaming hash on the table, and brought in a bowl of salad, and another of mashed potatoes that had been keeping hot in the oven. She poured soup into two bowls. 'And Bill will sit up with the sow.'

'Good. I'll ring in the morning.' Charles was hungry and

the soup was good. It warmed and it comforted. He attacked a huge piece of pasty with considerable appetite. He hadn't fed properly since breakfast. Nell passed him a dish of beetroot, and looked at her own plate. She felt sick with misery. She ate, hoping Charles wouldn't notice how little she was eating. Meg came to sit beside her and look up hopefully. She was never fed at human mealtimes but she always hoped something might fall by accident. Nell slipped a piece of meat off her plate and held it under the table. The bitch's soft lips closed on it, and she swallowed and went to Charles, to lean her head on his knee, telling him she'd missed him and why hadn't he taken her? She was never left behind.

'She's doing fine,' Charles said, looking down at the bitch. Her tail beat against his thigh.

There were raspberries from the deep freeze to follow. Nell was dedicated to her orchard and there was always soft fruit enough to last the winter. Cream from the one Jersey cow. And cream in his coffee. He was being spoilt tonight and it was a good feeling, in spite of the reason.

The grandfather clock in the corner ticked heavily, an insistent noise that went on for ever. The television set sat blankly. Not tonight, Nell thought. It's time and it's got to be done.

'Charles.'

He was fed and relaxed and sleepy.

'About Kate.'

'What about Kate?'

'You know what happened today,' Nell said, not knowing how to steer the conversation in the direction she needed. She had been angry with her daughter long before the ram died. It had taken hours to clean the milk stain from the carpet, and the carpet was almost new. It had been a birthday present for Kate.

'I should have moved Mackie before I went back to bed,' Charles said. 'Kate would assume I'd done it.'

'If you'd been Kate, with a ram that was new to the place, would you have put him into the field without checking every inch of it to make sure Mackie wasn't somewhere out of sight?' she asked. It was time Kate faced realities.

'It's easy to be wise by hindsight,' Charles said. 'Kate's obviously very upset or she'd have been home. But I wish she'd told me herself.'

'Rob could have stayed too,' Nell said acidly. 'As long as he's around Kate's going to have her head in the stars and no sense in her. He'll have to go.'

'What had Rob to do with it?' Charles asked. The men hadn't told him anything about Rob being there at the time.

'They were racing off to lunch together; they snatch every second they can to be alone when they're working and they're driving the men up the wall as neither of them is doing a fair share.' Nell wished her husband was more observant.

'I hadn't noticed. The men haven't complained,' Charles said.

'Not to you. I hear them talking when they come in for lunch; while I'm dishing up. They forget I have ears and that this room isn't soundproof. Rob will have to go, and it's time Kate stood on her own feet and not ours. Most girls her age are away from home, in a job, or married with a family to rear. We can give her the Baines's old cottage; you've been intending to do something with it for two years now, and it's deteriorating all the time it's empty. It'll do a double job: teach Kate to live alone, and be responsible for herself; and keep the cottage in good repair. And it's far enough away for her to be unable to come running home whenever things go wrong.'

Charles stared at his wife.

'What will she do for money? And for furniture? How will she live?'

'I've been thinking about that. Its three fields add up to about thirty acres. She can have six pullets to start her off; and four cows; with three in calf and a milker, she'll have eggs and butter and milk. She can rear her own chickens and kill them for the table. She can have a pair of geese; and a duck and a drake. There's a pond in the field by the house. It needs doing up, but that has to be done anyway, even if we sold the place. She can sell her calves and her baby chicks; she can think up ways of making herself self-sufficient. Old Baines had a good vegetable garden; she can grow enough for herself easily. We can give her twenty pounds a week for the first year: it's less than her wage would be, but she doesn't earn her wage here anyway. She treats it as pocket money; working for us is a job she puts down when she feels like it, if there's something more interesting to do.'

'She's young,' Charles said.

'We were young when war broke out. I was still at school. And a year later I was nursing, two years younger than Kate. I was nursing men coming home from the battle fronts; men with wounds that Kate couldn't even imagine; shell-shocked men; men destroyed by battle. Men who swore and ranted and raved. And before the war ended you were fighting too. What did we have when we married?' Nell had to make him understand. She hoped that Kate wouldn't come in too soon; they needed to work everything out, so that they could present her with facts.

Charles thought back over the years.

'A falling-down house that needed so much work done on it we spent half the time in despair; ten ewes and a not very good ram; ten elderly cows that never seemed to be in calf or give milk. And two babies. But we were older than Kate. We were both over thirty when we married.'

'We were both on our own when we were eighteen,' Nell said. 'Kate's nearly three years older than that. She'll be twenty-one before the year's out.'

'What about furniture?'

'There are a few bits and pieces there that I put in when you had that married farm student for the summer. She can save up for the rest, make do. We didn't have much to start with and I still haven't got what I want, only family pieces, and most of those are hideous. She can have all the things I loathe most. That dreadful rug in the dining room for a start. It doesn't match anything and the colours are revolting.'

'Sister Susie made that,' Charles said, grinning. His sister had the oddest taste in colours, putting together amazing clashes that no one else ever liked. As she made rugs for presents with most tremendous industry, Nell always hoped the rest of the family would be the recipients of her latest design. The last one she had received had been pleasantly plain, a hyacinth blue, that Kate had in her bedroom.

'Kate can have her bedroom furniture. And if she sold some of her more expensive clothes and her more exotic possessions she'd have something to start off with.'

'It sounds all very fine,' Charles said. 'I wonder how Kate will take it?'

'She's always wanted to be on her own.' Nell refused to face the fact that Kate's idea of being alone was a beautifully furnished little flat, with no work to do, and plenty of time and money to enjoy herself.

'When does she start this idyll?' Charles asked.

'As soon as possible.'

'You'll miss her,' Charles said.

'In a way, yes. In another, no. She makes more work than all the rest of you put together and she never helps in the house. Have you ever even had her make you a cup of tea?'

'I make my own if you're not there,' Charles said.

'Exactly. But Kate doesn't. She only has tea when someone else has made it and she can have a cup without the effort of boiling the water and pouring it on the tea.' Years of resentment suddenly boiled over.

'It would be nice to be on our own, Charles. Not to lie awake worrying myself sick when she's out half the night, wondering where she is and what she's doing; wondering if she's had an accident; been with someone who drank too much, who might crash his car and kill her in the process. Wondering what is going to happen next here, because she hasn't done something she should have done. You were out last week when Kate left the top field gate open; all the cows got on to the road and it was an hour before we knew it. Sergeant Lewis rang up to tell us. It took half the day to get them back. That's why the work was behind. But the men didn't want to tell tales about Kate, so they didn't say anything.'

'Suppose she tries it for six months? With us here to pick up the pieces. We can't just throw her out,' Charles said.

'No. But we don't interfere unless she asks us. And we leave her on her own. No advice unless she wants it. She knows enough of the basics of animal care; it's time she learned that no one but she is going to look after them. No one else to feed them if she forgets them; or to milk the cows; or to clean out when she wants to go dancing. She'll find out if she's cut out for farming. She might not be any more than Tim is. We've never really given her a choice, have we?'

There was never time to think of giving a choice. Charles leaned back and was about to speak when he heard the sound of a car turning slowly in the yard. The engine noise died. Minutes passed, and reluctant footsteps came towards the kitchen door.

The footsteps were too heavy for Kate. They paused and there was a quick knock.

'Come in,' Nell called.

Rob came in alone. His face was stiff with anger, his eyes bleak. He had had a severe shock, and it would be a long time before he forgot the day's events.

'Kate asked me to tell you she's staying the night with her friend Gillian, in her flat in Mancaster. She can't face her dad.'

Neither Nell nor Charles said anything. There didn't seem to be any reply.

'I want to apologise, not that that helps. I won't ever make a mistake like that again. But I think I ought to go somewhere else. I told Kate a lot of things I'm regretting, because she ought to have stayed and I ought not to have let her persuade me to go off. I hoped she'd see reason and come back with me. I'd like to go in the morning. But I'll help with the milking first.' Rob stood stiffly, miserable, waiting for Charles to answer.

'It would be better if you went,' Charles said at last. 'I should have moved Mackie before I went up to bed; it was partly my fault. I can't pretend I'm feeling noble and forgiving though, because I'm not, but we're all to blame.

And I can't forgive myself either for not being up when the ram came home.'

'It wasn't much to ask us, was it?' Rob said. 'We should have checked. I thought of doing it on the way back, reminding myself that the old boy would resent a newcomer . . . only . . .' He backed towards the door.

'Only . . . we all make mistakes, Rob,' Charles said. 'Have you had anything to eat this evening?'

'I've been driving around ever since I dropped Kate, plucking up courage to come back,' Rob said miserably.

'Come and eat,' Nell said. 'No use starving yourself. And it's not fair to expect Mrs. Tom to make a meal at this time. I've plenty of food in the house. You can have Kate's supper.'

Rob felt worse than ever.

'There's always food to spare here,' Nell said, meaning to hit hard while Rob was receptive. 'People go off without telling me they aren't going to be in, and I cook for seven and find I only have four to feed. Luckily it will deep freeze, but it means I've spent more time on the meal than I need have done.'

Rob looked at her. He had sat in the car in a lay-by, smoking, and thinking, and had not enjoyed his thoughts. He'd thought he loved Kate, but her cowardice had shocked him, and the quarrel that flared between them had angered him so much that in a brief few minutes he saw another girl; someone he had not even known existed, and he hadn't liked what he saw. She had no thought for her father, only pity for herself. It wasn't fair. She was a spoilt baby, not an adult at all, and he had been a fool. He should have done his job and got on with his work and earned his money. No wonder old Bill was forever shouting at him and the other men had little time for him. He looked hard at himself and didn't like what he saw.

'What will you do?' Charles asked. 'Do you want to farm?'

'I want to farm,' Rob said. 'I fell in love today with something that isn't even human . . . that ram . . . if I could rear beasts like that . . .' He stopped to eat and

57

swallow. 'I've never seen anything like it . . . that's why it was so hard to come back. To think he's dead . . .'

'We all need dreams.' Charles said. 'I'm starting again, hoping to find another as good; hoping to persuade Amby to let me have his young ram, once I've sorted out the finances on this one.'

'I couldn't be hard on him,' said Charles, when Rob had finally said goodbye, and the sound of his car engine had drifted away down the lane. 'He looked like death. He'll take a long time to live his misery down. And he has a farmer's eye for a beast. I think Rob's found himself.' Charles yawned. He'd had one hour's sleep in two days.

'I wish Kate had,' Nell said. It was going to be very hard to forgive her daughter, and the longer she stayed away, the harder it would become.

## CHAPTER SIX

◆◆◆◆◆◆◆

There was too much to do in the morning. Rob had gone and there was no sign of Kate. Though neither had worked hard enough, they had at least been there and had done many of the smaller jobs about the farm. Nell left the indoor work and went out to feed the calves, collect the eggs, and feed the orphan lambs. It was well past lunch time before there was time to pause and think.

'I'm going over to the cottage,' she said, catching Charles on his way to phone an order through for feed for the hens and the pigs. 'I'll give it a good airing, and sort it out. If Kate doesn't bother to get in touch with us, we'll go over and give her the key and take the animals over. She surely wouldn't leave beasts on their own?'

Charles didn't want to think about his daughter.

He nodded briefly and turned his mind thankfully back to his own problems. Kate had bitterly disappointed him, adding to her carelessness her refusal to come home and face them. She would be desperately miserable, he knew. And she had lost Rob as well. All the same . . .

Nell was glad to be doing something constructive. Worries were always worst when you had to sit back and endure and couldn't take action. A hare bounded down the road in front of her and she slowed, giving it time to collect its scattered wits and dart through the hedge. A lamb bleated in a field. She loved the spring. There were buds on the may tree, and celandines in the ditch.

She turned into Hangman's Lane. She had never thought about the name before, but now she saw it and was briefly uneasy. Willow Cottage, Hangman's Lane. They said the old hangman himself had lived there, over a hundred years ago and that the lane was haunted by the ghost of a girl who had stolen a horse and begged him for her life. The stump of the old gallows was in the hedge; they said horses shied and refused to pass it. Nell had visions of bodies swaying in the breeze and was glad it was light. Was it fair to let Kate live here on her own? It would be uncanny when it was windy, after dark. It was fair. Time Kate learned to grow up.

The hedges had not been cut for years. Trees hung over the lane, dripping water, as rain fell from a sullen sky. She would have to phone the electricity authority, make sure everything functioned, and make a note of repairs that needed doing. They should never have left the cottage empty so long, but day chased day with the relentlessness of a hound pack hunting down a fox.

She opened the door. The hinges creaked. Everything needed oiling. The place stank. A mangy cat dived past her into the garden, which was a tangle of last year's seedheads. A few early tulips pushed their way through grass that was harsh and straw dry. Inside, paper peeled off the walls. There was a damp patch in one corner, another on the ceiling and water had come through the roof. It was a hellhole and Nell's resolve faltered. She hadn't realised it

59

was quite so bad. She would clean it up. And then she thought of Kate, running away from reality, and decided to leave it. Kate could do it herself. It would do her good to learn how other people lived. She had never known struggle.

The kitchen was an apology of a room: a lean-to against the living room wall, the door connecting it almost off its hinges. There was a gas cooker that must have come out of the ark; it was practically an antique. Nell hadn't realised it was so old. She would replace that for Kate. The sink was stained, the outside brown glaze was cracked, the draining-board was wooden and rotten. The filthy window above it was broken. Nell itched to take hot water and make a start. She didn't intend to give way to her craving to put everything to rights, but she must prevent Charles from seeing it, or he would change his mind. It would be very good for Kate. Nell herself would have thought it fun when she was twenty. By then she had lived in a dozen horrible bed sitters, each worse than the last, in a dozen different towns with bombs raining down on Britain. She had married at thirty; and had her family late. Which had rejuvenated both of them. She and Charles always mixed with people younger than themselves, finding their contemporaries too elderly.

She drove home, and sat down at the kitchen table to make out a list. She was just completing it when the door opened and Kate walked in.

'I'm not coming back,' she said. 'I'm moving in with Gillian. It'll easy to find a job in Mancaster.'

'Dad and I decided it might be a good idea for you to have the Baines's cottage,' Nell said.

'That slum?' Kate's voice shook and she stared at her mother, appalled.

'You'd be on your own in the cottage; you can do as you like with it; decorate it as you like, furnish it as you like. Dad will give you some stock of your own and you can make your own life there. You can build it up, if you work hard enough on it.'

It wasn't easy to sound convincing. Nell was sure Kate would never manage to live by herself or cope alone.

Charles, coming into the room, heard the end of the sentence.

'Maybe she'd better stay here after all,' he said. 'I've been thinking it over. Kate can't manage alone; she's far too young and she would get into one hassle after another. We'll spend our lives driving over there to salvage her. It's an impossible idea. Maybe she'd be better going to Agricultural college. She's a lot to learn.'

'I can manage by myself perfectly,' Kate said, furious with her father. 'I won't need you to come and help me out. I'll show you. I don't want help. I'll show you what I can do without you, without either of you.'

She walked over to the door.

'I'm sorry about the ram,' she said, miserably. It was a terrible effort to speak the words and she didn't wait for an answer. They heard her quick feet racing up the stairs and the slam of her bedroom door.

'At least she came home and apologised,' Charles said.

## CHAPTER SEVEN
✦✦✦✦✦✦✦✦

Nell drove Kate over to Willow Cottage in the morning. One of the men would bring the Land Rover and trailer loaded with things she would need, when milking was ended. They sat, side by side, saying nothing at all. Nell had no idea what her daughter was thinking. She almost regretted her own decision when she saw the place again, and watched Kate walk up the weedy path and look around her.

'You can go now,' Kate said, wanting to be on her own, wanting to revel in misery. She never wanted to see either of her parents again. They obviously hated her, or they'd never have had such an unspeakable idea. And she'd lost Rob. She wished she was dead.

Nell sat in her car at the gate, looking at the front door, which Kate had closed firmly behind her. Kate had food for the day and buckets and cleaning cloths. The water and electricity were turned on. Nell drove away, feeling as if she had condemned her daughter to jail. The misery persisted all day and was not alleviated when Bill came back with the empty Land Rover trailer, having taken over Kate's possessions.

Kate had come to the door to greet him, her clothes filthy and her face grey with exhaustion.

'It's ghastly,' she said. 'It's only fit to burn down.'

She was revolted by the filth and she had never cleaned up anywhere so dirty before. Everything she cleaned seemed to need another clean. The cloths were so filthy she could only burn them. She washed the kitchen floor nine times before she could even see the pattern on the linoleum. She started on her bedroom, feeling she must have somewhere clean to sleep, and had to boil water to put in a basin to try and clean herself up. She hated being dirty. She felt she would never be clean again. The thought of Rob added to her misery. He had been hateful to her; it wasn't her fault Mackie had been in the field. She thought of the ram and shuddered. She hoped Bill would hurry; she wanted to be alone; she didn't want to see anybody, ever again.

How dared her parents make her live like this. How dared Rob say such things to her. It wasn't fair. She couldn't cook and she couldn't clean and she loathed housework. She hated washing and ironing and had a sudden appalled vision of herself spending day after day cleaning up and cleaning up again, washing, ironing, baking, no freedom, with the animals to care for as well. It would be slavery. And nobody could live on twenty pounds a week. Would her father pay the rates? And the animal feed bills?

Bill brought in the last load and put it down on the floor.

'Be all right?' he asked.

'Of course,' Kate said, with immense dignity, and Bill grinned to himself as he went out, a feeling of pity behind the grin. Poor little devil; she didn't know what had hit her, but it was about time. His girl had been married two years and had twin babies and a husband that was a fair handful, gambling his money away so that Sally had to budget and make sure Dick didn't have too much in his pocket, and she was a year younger than Kate. The cottage was as bad as this, or had been when Sal and Dick moved in. Though he hadn't wanted Sally to marry at seventeen.

He'd bet a week's wages that Kate would be home with her tail between her legs in a few weeks, asking to come back. Too flighty by half, silly little wench. And never did her share of work either, flirting with young Rob all the time and distracting him from his job. Brought it on herself.

He dismissed Kate from his thoughts and went back to get on with the evening milking, cursing heartily as Arabellina shoved him hard against the wall, in one of her flightier moods.

Kate finished cleaning her bedroom, and tried to light the kitchen fire. It was a big old-fashioned hearth, the grate black, the chimney breast hooded. She went outside to see if there was any wood. The trees grew thick and close, and with the coming of dusk the lane was shaded and alarming. A body rustled in the grass. A cat leaped to a gatepost and glared at her, spitting. There were lights across the field; a biggish house by the look of it, at least within sight, which made her feel less isolated. Looking along the horizon she made out the bulk of two barns, and a haystack. Somewhere not too far away a horse whinnied.

She found wood and returned to the cottage. The paint was peeling off the door in long strips. She prised one away with her finger nail. It looked as if the wood were rotten underneath.

Rain began.

She stood uncertain, not knowing what to do next. There was so much to do. Too much to do. Every room was deep in grime; some of the windows were broken and all were filthy and covered in cobwebs. The bathroom contained a vast white bath on clawed legs, the inside stained with rust; a cracked washbasin, filled with dead leaves that had drifted in through the window, and an antiquated lavatory with a large wooden seat. She pulled the chain. That at least worked. There was no plug for the basin or the bath, and when she bent to look at the floor, she saw that the ancient linoleum was coming to pieces.

There was little comfort downstairs, even with the fire lit and the table scrubbed. The peeling wallpaper hung in shreds, and the place smelled musty. It also smelled of cats, and she found evidence of them in the second bedroom where a dead bird and half a mummified rabbit revolted her so much she couldn't face any food at all. Bill had brought enough provisions for a week when he came with her possessions.

The rain had turned to sleet.

She could not face indoors—not yet.

She walked to the fence that enclosed the kitchen garden and looked over the field. It stretched to the river, flooding over the banks, lying below her. It couldn't flood right up here, or could it?

There were old fruit trees in the garden, standing in tangled grass that hadn't seen a mower for several years.

There was a derelict shed, with only half a roof. There was an old stable, without a door. Inside the floor held straw and a stink she couldn't identify until three chickens flew out of the corner. They must have been living here wild. There were the remains of eggs on the floor. Rats? Or cats? Or stray dogs? She didn't know. It would have to be cleaned and scoured and made fit for a mare. She would buy a mare. A beautiful mare of her own.

She held to the thought as if it were a mascot for her future.

There was an old barn, filled with incredible rubbish; a mangle that had come from the ark; a zinc wash tub with a wooden dolly inside; a broken electric iron and two flat irons. An old glazed sink. She swallowed at the thought. She leaned on the broken gate, seeing nothing. She had never felt so alone in her life.

None of her friends would help. They'd all make the proper noises and go away, as they danced saying 'Did you hear about Kate Malone? How about that then?' and laugh again and forget her. And she'd have no money to spare, ever again.

She couldn't stay here all night. She was frozen. Colder than she had ever been before. She was filthy and needed a bath and there was no chance of a bath. She'd have to wash all over; she'd stand by the fire to keep warm, using a basin. She wanted a hot drink. Bill had put several cartons down in the kitchen. She found bread and milk and eggs and bacon and a big pasty in the first, and in the second a couple of saucepans, a frying pan and a new electric kettle. Gratefully she filled it and plugged it in. The fire burned with a sulky glow and the room was murky with smoke. There was probably a nest in the chimney. There was an electric fire in the corner, also new. Her mother must have been out shopping and that would have taken all the afternoon. They lived a long way from any major shops.

Kate plugged in the fire, and knelt to warm her hands by it, and then turned in terror at the thump of footsteps in the pantry. She watched the door, afraid to move. Slowly, carefully, a black and white cat came into the room. Kate was so relieved she laughed and flicked a finger at it.

'Have I taken your home? Come and have some milk then.'

She poured milk into a saucer and watched it drink. It was filthy and one ear flicked, as if it suffered from continuous irritation. She was glad of its company and amused when, its milk finished, it licked its paw and washed its face, and then curled in front of the electric fire, its rusty purr throbbing.

It could be company. The place was lonely. She had never been alone in any house before. There were always people around, and if her parents went away, Tom and his wife came and slept in, and looked after her. Mrs. Tom always spoilt her.

She sat down to eat, listening to the wind as it screeched

round the house. It was a desolate sound that matched her mood. She would never enjoy living here; she would never manage on her own. Her father was right.

As she ate, her mood improved. She would show her parents she could live alone. All the same, she put off going to bed, and as she left the room and turned out the light, she thought dismally that here she was with a rented cottage, as she had discovered she had to pay rent out of the money her father was giving her, as well as keep herself and the animals, and all she had was a few expensive possessions that were no use at all, and a stray cat.

She lay in bed, aching with misery. Her hands were raw, the varnish chipped. She always took such care of her nails. She lay staring at a curved new moon, wondering whether to get up and dress again and go to the phone box down the lane and beg to come home. She couldn't stand it here alone at night. The leaves rustled and the wind howled and there were owls screeching in the dark. There were footsteps on the stairs.

She lay listening, and then sighed with relief as she heard a mew. She had forgotten the cat. It felt cold when the fire was turned off, and was seeking warmth. It had been dumped when its owners moved away from the estate in the town, and it remembered people who gave it food and comforted it, even though they had turned it out in the end, moving to a flat and not allowed to have animals. They hadn't wanted to put it to sleep and thought they were doing it a kindness in giving it life, in a country place where mice were sure to be around in plenty.

It jumped onto Kate's bed. She stroked it. It needed to be cleaned up and it was insane to have it there, but at least it was something else alive and close and near. She was too tired to care. She lay for a long time, sleep evading her, and finally put on her dressing gown and went downstairs again, thankful to switch on the light, and to put on the fire, and to boil the kettle. The cat came down and she gave it a bowl of cornflakes. It was an odd shape, its belly bloated and the rest of it thin. The fur was harsh; it had been living wild and fed itself badly. It probably had worms as well.

It was better to think of the cat, to fasten on to small thoughts, than to give way to desolation. She couldn't stop thinking of her room at home. Warm, centrally heated, clean, because her mother kept it spotless. The carpet was soft underfoot. The linoleum was icy but maybe she would find a rug tomorrow. She hadn't bothered to look and see what Bill had brought.

She made cocoa. Her mother was a cocoa person, she thought with amused and wry affection and grinned at herself, feeling a little better. There was a large biscuit tin, and when she opened it, among the homemade buns and scones, was a tiny parcel, wrapped in patterned paper and tied with a ribbon.

She undid the wrapping and was back in memory at the farm; herself with measles and a promise her mother had made that as soon as she could eat again she could have a bar of mint chocolate, which she adored. She had been very small. After that, mint chocolate had been a kind of secret signal, between the two of them. Her apology to her mother always consisted of buying a bar, wrapping it and tucking it into Nell's folded nightie for her to find last thing at night. Kate's own forgiveness from her mother was also always tucked up on her pillow.

She looked at the bar, and put it on the draining board, as a message to herself. Her mother knew how she felt.

It was too cold upstairs. She brought down her blankets, and laid them on the floor. It was cleaner here, as well as warmer. She had her sleeping bag too. There was a fireguard that she put in front of the heater, and curled herself up on the hard boards, leaving the light on for comfort, looking at the bar of chocolate as if it were a talisman to conjure away fear. She was cold. Cold with misery; cold with exhaustion; cold with rejection.

She was frightened, as there were noises in the lane. The windows were no protection. Half of them were broken and in spite of cardboard tacked across the panes in the bedroom the wind had roared in, ice on its breath.

Suppose there was a drunk out there, or an escaped prisoner, or a peeping Tom? Or a tramp who used the cottage and didn't know it was now occupied and insisted on sharing it with her. She was glad the light was on. She looked at her watch. Two o'clock and a long way to morning. The cat had come downstairs with her; at least she had that. It mewed and she suddenly realised its bloated appearance was due to kittens. She had assumed for some reason that it was a male, possibly because it was so ugly, poor brute.

Kittens would be fun. The farm cats were allowed to breed and she adored playing with their litters. They teased straws and chased her finger and were warm and soft and purry. There would be mice here, and rats, and she'd need cats. She could keep them all.

If they survived the birth. The cat was in such dreadful condition and she couldn't have had much scavenging here. Kate sat up and whistled and the cat came across to her. She really was in appalling shape. There was an abscess on her jaw, and her face was swollen; it had broken recently. It needed treatment.

Kate pulled on trousers and jersey and heated water again and bathed the injury. This was insane. She needed sleep but sleep refused to come. She made her bed again. The floor was hard and she thought of going back to the bedroom, but the wind through the broken windows was more than she could bear; it was freezing hard outside, and there was a film of ice on the water on the pantry windowsill, leaked from a missing tile. Spring had vanished and winter had returned. The blossom in the orchard would be killed.

Kate bathed the abscess and cleaned the ears. She must get drops to put in. She found a cardboard box in the kitchen, under the draining-board. She lined it with one of her tee shirts and put the cat inside.

She was thankful to creep back to bed and lie between the warm covers.

She was at last too tired to care about the noises in the trees. An owl called and was answered, but Kate didn't hear. She slept, forgetting her aching muscles and her misery.

She wakened to darkness. Day was a long way off still. The cat was pawing at her arm, a desperate pawing that would not be denied. She crept out of bed and found the light switch. She looked at her watch. Half past five. The cat was trying to give birth and the first kitten seemed to have jammed half way. Kate had delivered lambs. She eased the kitten out; she warmed more milk and relighted the fire. The cat settled to wash the kit, licking it obsessively, nudging it against her, delighted that it was there.

Four more kittens were born, without further need for Kate's help. She tucked cat and kittens in the box, as near to the electric fire as was safe.

She went back to bed.

She woke to daylight. There was a weight against her. Cat and kittens had moved in, under the top blanket, and lay there snug and warm. It wasn't exactly hygienic. Kate began to laugh. The wild laughter echoed from the walls, pulsed in the room, and the cat sat up and stared at her. Kate had begun her career already. She had six cats.

She dressed by the fire, hating the chill in the cottage. It hadn't been warmed for years. There was frost outside on the unkempt grass. She'd have to see to the chimney. Electricity was too expensive.

Kate needed groceries: cat food, vitamins for the cat, milk for the kittens—the cat couldn't possibly feed them properly in her condition. She was a gentle animal, black and white, with white socks, white face, and black whiskers, an appealingly anxious expression on her face, as if she expected to be evicted.

'I wouldn't turn you out for all the world,' Kate told her, as she put down more bread and milk. 'I know what it feels like."

Kate began to sort her possessions. She could sell her watch; and her radio, which was expensive and almost new, and buy a cheap transistor; that would be company.

Money.

There was ten pounds in an envelope on the mantelpiece, tucked behind a clock that the Baines's must have left behind them. Most of their belongings had gone. There had been a farmhand in here for a few months, when Kate thought back. She hadn't noticed the envelope.

'A bonus; love, Mum.'

It would be a big help. Kate had always spent her wages; petrol, meals out, clothes, cosmetics; there had been no need to save. She lived at home, and had no expenses. Now did her father pay the rates or must she? She didn't know.

It was almost eight o'clock and there was so much to do. She would have to start or nothing would ever be done.

Milk for the cat.

The kittens were small domed heads, and blindly sucking mouths, surprisingly noisy. They looked fit and well, in spite of their bad start. The mother needed attention; she was starvation thin and it wouldn't do to feed her too much too soon or she'd be upset and might die on them.

Kate cut bread for toast. The cooker was old and the grill was slow. There was butter, no marmalade—the bare basics for a few days. She looked in her purse. She had eighteen pounds left from her last week's wages. She never had tried to save money. There was always more and she paid nothing for her keep. She had never thought about it. How much did bread cost? And she'd nowhere to put the cows; she'd need to find help with that. She'd twenty-eight pounds, with her mother's money.

She glanced uneasily at the clock. She had to go on putting the cottage to rights. Even after scrubbing the floor so much it didn't look clean. The wallpaper hung from one corner of the wall. It was revolting paper, bright red roses on a puce background. It would have to come off. She'd distemper the walls; or did you whitewash? She didn't know. She didn't know anything. A dog barked in the distance. She'd get a dog. It would be both company and protection. You could talk to a dog without feeling a fool, as they needed to be spoken to. No other way you could tell them they were doing right or wrong.

It would follow her round all day.

It would be company in the evenings too. She wasn't going to have money to spare to go out, to travel, to visit friends or even ask people in. She had to learn a whole new way of life and she was scared, deep down, afraid that her father was right and she just wasn't adequate.

She'd need the cattle to graze the fields. No other way of keeping the grass down and she certainly couldn't manage to plough them and sow them. Maybe there was room for a store bullock or two. Farming on her own . . . that would be adventure. There would be point to it, making money by it, making a living for herself, making money to buy a mare; maybe she could rent more fields once she made a go of it.

The place was totally dead except for the little cat. She'd always been used to so many animals. She soaked bread in milk again and fed it to the cat who sucked it greedily. The mother left the kittens briefly and walked outside, to dig a hole and squat, her back modestly turned to Kate, amusing her. An industrious muscular paw filled the hole with earth, and the cat came in again, taking a detour to weave round Kate's legs and purr, and then settling in the box again, nudging each head against her, licking each kit clean.

Three of the kittens were black and white. The other two were long haired, blue black, almost true Persians. Just now they were unreal, uncatlike, with spiky tails and bullet heads, ears almost flat. It would be intriguing to watch them grow, and here in her own house there was no one to say they couldn't stay indoors.

Kate could do as she liked.

She would have chickens. Bantams maybe. Or something exotic and more interesting than the usual breeds. Eggs. She could never kill the birds for the table. She hated that. She hated the spring lambs going to market and she never ate veal—rearing veal calves was horrible, not even her father would do it. She had seen the bobby calves stagger into the slaughterhouse, almost before they could walk. No calf of hers would end like that.

Her mood was lighter, though behind it was still depression when she stopped to think. She could never cope; never manage alone; would have to find another kind of job. She looked at the cottage. There was too much to be done. No curtains, dirty windows, that terrible wallpaper and worse in the other rooms.

Maybe when she'd settled in and made this place into

something halfway decent her mother would come over for a meal; she'd cook her something special.

Making plans—they alternated with moods of depression.

By the weekend the room was stripped of paper, and she had covered the walls with white paint. It looked amateurish and depressing. Perhaps paper would be better but it wouldn't hang right.

Nothing seemed to work.

The grill burned the bread or failed to turn it more than pale gold when she made toast.

Nor would it grill bacon properly and Kate had relied on a pound of bacon to make her several meals. She stewed it, but the stew was tasteless; its only virtue was that it was hot. She had never worked so hard in her life. She had never been so tired in her life.

Every evening found her exhausted. She had bought her little transistor radio. The place was comfortless. There wasn't time to make curtains; there wasn't time to think of buying anything to brighten up the shelves.

She took all day to do jobs that her mother did in half the time and even then it didn't look right. Cooking took so long; and the bus journey into town for food took the whole of one morning. She ate in a café and spent a pound on a meal that she couldn't afford and that wasn't worth the money—egg and chips, bread and ice cream and coffee. She bought a four ounce jar of instant coffee. The price horrified her.

Even a tin of cat food cost twenty pence.

By Tuesday evening Kate had only a few pence left; and nothing to show for her outlay except paper and paint, turps to remove the stains she made on the floor, and cat food and the barest essentials for herself. A dozen eggs had cost fifty-four pence; one egg would have to do for an omelette but that left her hungry. Meat was too expensive. Kate bought four sausages in the supermarket, and ignored the glance of the girl who served her. She didn't want to shop where she was known.

She felt as if everyone were talking. Kate Malone's been thrown out.

She couldn't afford a dog; it would cost too much to feed.

She was sure she could never manage. She went up to bed and lay awake, prices and odd details running through her head. She woke after only two hours' sleep with a blinding headache and a sick feeling that she was going to fail, that she was unable to cope in any way. She felt shivery and her throat ached. Had she been at home she would have stayed in bed, expecting her mother to nurse her; to bring her hot drinks and perhaps to ring the doctor.

Now she was on her own.

It was useless staying in bed; no one would come.

Kate felt dizzy, but the dizziness passed when she drank coffee. She could not eat food. She could not face the cottage; she washed the dishes left over from the night before, fed the cat, and took her coat. Perhaps if she went out for the day everything would be better in the evening and she would feel well again. She'd been overworking.

She sneezed as she put on her coat.

Only a cold, maybe.

The place was damp, and it was so cold at night, even with extra bedding.

There was only one place she could go to without spending money—the Beast Sale. Kate loved the Sales, looking at the cattle, looking at the sheep, and above all looking at the horses. Now she knew her desire for a mare was a pipe dream, never to come true. She hadn't enough money to keep herself and the cat, let alone buy a horse and have that to feed; and vet bills. The cat ought to see the vet. That would cost money. Was there anything in the world that didn't cost money? She hadn't even enough for the bus. She stood at the end of the lane, hoping for a lift.

Rain was falling again. It seemed to have been raining ever since she had come to live in the lane. Hangman's Lane. She looked at the name and shivered. The old gallows had stood here, long ago. Were there ghosts? She didn't know. The pick-up that stopped for her was driven by an elderly man.

'Come on in out of the rain,' he said. 'You're the girl at Willow Cottage aren't you? We're almost neighbours. I'm

73

manager at the Brayshaw Stud Farm. I'm off to the Beast Sale; there's a horse we're interested in. Might be useful. I'm Ted Holloway.'

'I'm Kate Malone,' Kate said. She was feeling shivery and a bit light headed and thought that a limerick could start with Brayshaw and Malone, but the thought drifted away. She should have stayed at home. She'd heard of Mr. Brayshaw. He bred racehorses.

She had nothing to say.

She looked out at the rain, answering only briefly when Ted asked where he could drop her.

'I'm going to the Beast Sale too,' she said.

She was crazy.

Kate thanked him as he parked the car, and sneezed again. It was going to be one snorter of a cold. And she hadn't time to have a cold. Please heaven it wasn't flu. She'd feel better once she got to the sale ring, sitting there, watching and listening, caught up in the excitement.

She huddled into her coat. At least that was warm; a thick sheepskin coat her mother had given her for her birthday two years ago. She wondered if her mother would give her presents any more. Perhaps they had cut her off with a pittance, for ever. She forced her way through the crowd. All the world and his wife seemed to come to the Show. Farmers with collies at heel, their wives sheepskin-coated beside them; old men, young men, gypsies, looking at the horses, maybe selling a horse. A brown-eyed dark-haired man with one gold earring showing under his curly hair grinned at her. A horse danced by, showing its paces. Cattle lowed in the pens and the place stank of pigs.

Kate felt sick. She shouldn't have come. She should have stayed in bed. She forced her way into the main part of the building where the horses stood in stalls, each one marked by a red lot number on the rump. She felt better, just looking at them. One day, she would buy a mare. She walked on, slowly, patting one, stroking another, speaking to a man who stood beside his charge. She forgot time and forgot her cold.

And then she saw something that stopped her completely and took away her breath. . . .

74

# CHAPTER EIGHT

It was the last time.

The last time he would wake in this house; the last time he would look at the furniture that he and Mary had bought when they married; the last time he would walk in the fields that had never been his fields. If he had had the money he would have bought the farm, would have owned his land and this would never have happened.

He could still see the cold faces of the men who had come to assess his last year's work. Young men, brash men, seeing in front of them a man who had had his life; bent, worn, marked with years. Eighty years. It didn't seem like that. He had lived too long, outlasted his friends, outlasted his wife.

Joe could remember Mary without regret. She had been a good wife; and he had not known, until she died and left him alone, just how much she meant to him. He had never said. Life was full of regrets; of the wrong thing said; and never the right thing. He paused to look at the photograph of Ellie. Even now, it brought pain.

He could remember the day Ellie was born, as if it were yesterday; he had been milking when Mary came to the byre, clutching at him, so that the milk stream shot over his boots instead of into the bucket. No fancy milking machines then. Ellie would be over fifty now. It didn't seem possible.

He had delivered foals and horses, but never a baby before. There wasn't time to go down the road to the phone. He had it all to do, alone. He had held the baby as she came; an extension of himself, yelling, red-faced, but beautiful. Joe had done all that should be done, and wrapped the child in a shawl, made his wife comfortable, and then gone down the road to ring the doctor and the nurse.

Ellie had meant more to him than the boys; she had grown into a beautiful child; into a girl who laughed at him and teased him. She had helped him plant the daffodils for Mary's Christmas present. It was to be a surprise. A golden drift under the willow tree, greeting her, as near to her birthday as possible. They had given her a picture drawn by Ellie, of the drift of flowers as they hoped it would be.

Ellie had loved the horses as much as he loved them, handling the big Shires better than any man, grooming them, walking them, sitting with him when he nursed them, standing beside him when they were foaling, kneeling in the straw to look at the new foal, assessing its shape as it grew, coming with him when he judged, always with him when she was not at school. She worked beside him, mucking out, nothing too heavy for her.

He could still hear her laugh, see the way she tossed her head and the blonde pony tail flashing in the air like a horse's mane. She remained, for ever, at twenty. She had been leaving him then, and going out with John. He liked John, the son of a farmer down the lane. A good boy who would make a good farmer, a good husband, a good man.

He poured coffee from the old brown pot.

The last time.

The toast was slightly burned but he did not taste it. Ellie laughed at him from the silver frame. He could remember every moment of that day. They had moved the foals and mares to the big field. She had come in, just before evening milking, in a new dress she had made herself. She was clever with her fingers, like her mother. She and John were going dancing.

'Enjoy yourself,' he had said, and had meant it. He wanted her to be happy, to grow away from him, live her own life, but to bring him her children. Mary had worried because they were late and he had laughed at her. Young people out alone on a moonlit night; they were always late. He could remember the car drawing up at the gate. The slow heavy footsteps. The expression on the policeman's face. A young policeman; his first time ever, bringing bad news, almost in tears.

A drunk, driving blindly out of a side road. He and Martin had gone together to look at their dead children. Ellie would never see the daffodils they had planted. It was the only thought in his head, as he looked at his daughter for the last time.

He moved heavily, washing up the plate, the cup, the saucer, concentrating because it was not always easy to remember everything these days. Yesterday, and the yesterdays of long ago were more vivid and sometimes he felt Ellie was waiting for him, and they would meet again in fields where his long-gone horses and dogs also played. It was a thought to hold on to, a thought that took away fear. Waiting for the last door to open, to find what was on the other side. He believed in God, but it was hard to understand God's ways. Sometimes the old man felt the world was a joke, played by a cruel tyrant, on creatures he thought beneath contempt, so that he laughed at their struggles and their posturing, their miseries and fears.

Joe would take his photographs and the little desk; he couldn't take much to the Home. He didn't want to go. The Staff with their quiet professional smiles, switched on and off, had all had cold eyes and, though it was bright and clean and the food looked good, it wasn't the same as home. He wouldn't be alone, ever, not even at night. He hadn't the money to pay for privacy. They'd take his pension and give him pocket money, like a little boy again.

He had been alone since Mary died and the boys went away; Paul to Canada, where he now had his own ranch; and Mark to New Zealand, where he was manager to a sheep farmer who numbered his flock in thousands. Joe was a great-grandfather now. He'd only photographs of the babies.

An old man's dreams of the years behind 'ee,
Your darter's youngest darter to mind 'ee . . .

It didn't do to remember. He went outside. There was nothing left in the yard. He had sold the hens and sold the cows. A whinny greeted him from the stable, and he went, dragging his feet, to open the door, and let the Queen see the morning air. For the last time.

His January Queen, born in the snow, her foaling long and difficult, the last of all his mares. Eight years ago and she herself in foal now. He would never have mated her had he known another man would have to foal her. He couldn't take a horse to the Home. A Shire mare, even with the best of breeding, as the Queen had, had no place there. He'd hoped My Lady might have her but My Lady was abroad, judging dog shows in Australia.

Usually he whistled as he groomed the Queen, and talked to her, telling her the little silly things there was no one else to tell—a brown egg from the hen that had never laid an egg in her life, about to be killed for his Sunday meal and now reprieved; the little new calf in the end byre. The end byre mocked him with its silence.

He had spent hours the day before, polishing her till her coat shone. He wanted a good buyer, a man who would love her as he had loved her and who would treasure her foal. The harness was ready, every brass gleaming; the little flags stood proud in her braided mane and tail; gay little flags, red and yellow flags, bright as the bright ribbons he had threaded the night before, not wanting to leave her ready for show, but knowing today there would not be time. He had gone to bed at four, to sleep briefly, a cat doze, waking in the dark, knowing that this was the last time he would do any of the things he loved doing.

He led the mare outside. It was a bright day, but there were clouds on the horizon and clouds over the dying elms. Elm disease would change the face of his land as it changed bigger farms and better homes. Everything old was dying.

He hated the world he now lived in. Long ago, when there had been horses, and men walked more slowly and time and money were not gods, life had been good. Now, men threw bombs to kill babies because of strange causes that had no reality; men could not work as he had once worked. A day's work for a day's pay had always been his motto and if the men he had employed in his old age had been half the man he had been, he would not be leaving now.

He knew the farm was slipping downhill, its care beyond him, but there should have been young men to work for him. Those who had come had cheated him, by leaving the job when they were most needed; by ignorance and stupidity and sloth. There wasn't time to bewail his lot. He would take his Bible; there would be time for reading; too much time, days going by punctuated only by meals. He would not last long, when the Queen had gone. She was his only reason for living.

She had nudged him with her nose, wanting her food. He brought her nosebag. He had to clean the stable. He would not be coming back, but he couldn't leave it dirty. He worked until it was as spotless as if new made.

The Land Rover and horse box drove into the yard. Morning was just beginning; dawn brightening the sky. The auction was to be held in the next town.

'Ready, Joe?' Les Masters asked. He was a big man, his clothes tight on his body, a hard man pushing forty, but as he saw the mare, beribboned for a show, he caught his breath and inside him his mind screamed in pity. Christ, the poor old bastard. Readied for a fair and like to be sold for a song; today would kill the old man.

'Coming inside with me?' he asked, though he knew the answer. Joe Makin had already opened the horse box, put up the ramp and was leading the mare inside, his face set and bleak. He couldn't speak. He shook his head.

Sitting in the straw, looking at the gleaming feather round the mare's hooves, he tried to make his mind a blank, but Ellie had come into it that morning and refused to be evicted. She was almost as real as the mare and it was hard to think she would be a middle-aged woman, nothing like the girl he knew. This next year, he wouldn't see the daffodils either. He hoped the new tenants wouldn't dig them up. There was a lawn full of them now, glowing in the sunshine under the trees, and they had

79

given Mary so much pleasure. Pleasure had been hard to find for a long time after Ellie died.

It was no consolation to know that the man who hit the car had been crippled for life. Martin had sold his farm soon after; he had no son to carry on. He and Sally had gone to Australia, had lived there for many years and now they too were dead.

The journey ended too soon.

He led the mare out and through the strawy ground to her stall. A man in a brown overall slapped a number on her rump, startling her, so that she stamped a hoof and he quieted her, shh girl, easy easy, little girl.

She wasn't little, she towered over him, but she had been his little girl from foaling. Her mother had died only last year. She was of good breeding, taken to a good stallion, carrying a good foal. It must make a difference; someone would buy her. He didn't care about the money. He wanted a good home.

Beyond him in the ring, the auction had started. He could hear the quick singsong lilt, the glib patter, the carrying voice calling the prices, eyes catching eyes, lifted hands and nodding heads and twitched fingers. He had bid in the ring himself. 'What am I bid, am I bid, am I bid? Twenty-five, and thank you sir, and forty-five and thank you mam, a higher bid, a higher bid; who's for fifty-five, sixty-five I'm bid, I'm bid, seventy-five and thank you sir, and did you say eight, eighty-five.' The voice was a bitter reminder of his coming fate.

Lot 55.

They would be in early; before lunch. And he would go home alone, and pack his few things and be driven round to the Home. He would lock the door and hand over the key. He'd walk and talk and eat and drink. They wouldn't know he had died, here in the auction room when his mare was sold.

If only he could die. Quickly, mercifully, not knowing what would happen to her, fearing the worst, hoping against hope. No one wanted Shires now; not here, though they would come into their own again; he knew that. People passed and smiled at the mare in her bravery. They couldn't see into his mind. He stared back, stony-faced, and they thought him a sour old man, not knowing they were looking at the end of his world.

A girl came round the corner and his heart pounded suddenly. She walked easily, her pony tail swinging free. Ellie come to life. But it wasn't Ellie. Brown eyes met his, instead of blue; the curve of the cheek was different, her hair was dark and there was something in her face that pulled at him; there was desolation in her eyes, so that she looked at him, and recognised the terror inside him.

She stopped to look at the horse. Such a horse. He saw the look on her face—the instant love, the passion.

'She's beautiful,' the girl said.

She couldn't walk away. She wanted the horse. It was an idiotic want. She needed the horse, and she saw the swelling lines.

'She in foal?'

Joe nodded.

The attendant was waiting.

Lot 55.

He led the mare down the ramp and under the spotlight. People smiled at her, dressed in her bravery just to be sold. What a quaint idea. Still, she looked pretty and it made a change. Joe was beside her, his face a mask hiding terror. The worst that could happen . . . he didn't dare to think.

The girl was at the ringside. She was looking at the mare as if she would eat her. Perhaps she would bid for her; with her, she would have a home and someone who loved her. The Queen had always had the best of everything: a warm stable at night, straw to bed on, and all his attention. She was more than a horse; she had been his companion for these past years, since his other horses died. Horses had been his life.

Long ago, his first judging appointment, and the mare that took his breath away. The Queen's Glory. He had judged her best in show and he had bought her foal—the Queen's Treasure. They had all been Queens, his mares. The Treasure had won prize upon prize. He would take his rosettes to his room to remind him, and his press cut-

81

ting books, and his photograph albums; he would have to sit and remember the past. An old man, no longer of use to the world, tidied away till he died. He didn't want to listen to the bidding. It was better to drift away in a haze.

The bidding had stopped.

Incredibly, the hammer was going down, once, twice and again.

'All done, for seventy pounds.'

Seventy pounds.

He turned his head to look at the man going up to the attendant, a roll of fivers in his hand. The knacker. His mare had been sold for meat. He stumbled out of the ring. The girl was standing silent.

'Who bought her?' she asked.

He didn't answer.

He was praying to his God to end his life then and there with a swift and merciful blow, stopping his heart so that he could not feel the pain. But his God was deaf and didn't hear.

Behind him the merciless patter had started again.

# CHAPTER NINE

Kate recognised the desolation on his face.

Seventy pounds for a Shire mare in foal. They were fetching a fortune in America; she knew that, from listening to the talk of her friends who bred horses. They were thinking of starting in Shires. It couldn't be true. She watched the old man. He was beside the mare, walking proudly, but she had seen his eyes. He wasn't going to show his feelings. Now or ever.

His mare was about to die.

He had one last request, when he found his voice and he found the knacker. He would shoot her himself; that way, she would not know fear. He would take her home, back to the familiar stable, for a few last nights; and then the man could come for the carcase. She wasn't going to end her days in a knacker's yard among strangers, with no one to care. He would ask for another week, before handing over. He'd been moving early.

He couldn't bear to do it, but it would be better to do it himself. And he knew that when he had done he would be tempted to load the gun again . . . and use it. Nothing was real any more. Ellie called to him from a buttercup field; a little girl, running, her sunbonnet slipping backwards off her head; one tooth missing.

'Let me ride the May Queen, please, daddy.' He had swung her on to the broad back and the May Queen had looked at the little girl, turning her wise head, her foal imminent. Ellie had been a featherweight; only five, with a gap in her teeth and freckles. Perhaps memory would take over and let him forget the present.

Kate watched him go.

The mare vanished, her flags flying bravely, her regalia outstanding amongst the crowd. She walked proudly, regally, as if being shown; men always admired her and to-day, for her, was no different. She was with her owner. She trusted him completely. She had never known anyone else tend her.

'Who bought that mare?' Kate asked the man beside her. She hadn't seen the buyer. Her view was blocked.

He wasn't interested and turned away.

She sneezed and began to shiver.

Her head was pounding, a small merciless hammer beating inside her brain, making it impossible to think. She felt a wave of nausea pass over her and stood against the wall, wishing she were in her bed. People pushed past her.

A man trod on her foot.

There was another horse in the ring now, a small chestnut mare; there was an aura of excitement, and the bidding suddenly registered on her mind. 'A thousand guin-

eas, I'm bid, I'm bid; a thousand and fifty, a thousand
one hundred; twelve hundred I'm bid, I'm bid.' It was a
fast singsong, and the crowd were coming closer to the
ringside, those sitting were standing, those at the back had
climbed onto bales of straw as the bidding rose higher and
higher. 'Fifteen thousand guineas—any advance on fifteen, thank you sir . . .' the voice went on, ringing in her
head.

It might have been like that for the mare.

She wondered if the old man needed the money.

She wondered why he was selling an animal he obviously treasured so much. Perhaps it wasn't his; perhaps
he was the groom who had tended her for all her life. She
sneezed again, and the ring swam out of focus, and Kate
sat down. She felt feverishly hot. She had to go. She
pushed through the crowds, wondering if she would manage to get home at all. She should never have come. A boy
ran past her, licking at a ball of candyfloss. The sight revolted her. At last she was out in the street.

She needed to get home, but how? She counted the pen-
nies in her purse. Enough to get her three-quarters of the
way and then she would have to walk. The bus journey
was a nightmare. Her throat ached and she alternated between feeling far too hot, and violent shivering fits. The
conductor stopped to look at her, white teeth gleaming
momentarily in a coffee-coloured face.

'You all right, miss?' he asked.

'I think I've got flu,' Kate said.

'Where do you live?'

'Down Hangman's Lane.' It sounded as remote as
Mars. Over a mile to walk. She'd never make it.

'You only booked part way.' His voice was concerned.
The girl looked dreadful.

'I hadn't enough money.'

He dipped into his pocket and brought out fifteen
pence, and rolled off another ticket.

'That will take you nearer home. Pay me when you
come again.'

He went off before she could thank him. She sat, endur-
ing, until the bus stopped at the corner of the lane.

'You got someone to help you?'

Kate nodded. No use saying no. He couldn't do anything for her, and she didn't care anyway. All she wanted was to get home and lie down. One foot in front of another, very carefully. In through the creaking gate. And into a room where dead ashes lay in the hearth, where the ceiling was half decorated and where the cat mewed, wanting food.

Kate put part of a tin of rabbit for cats into the saucer and went up to her bed. Nothing mattered any more. She felt better when she woke, but her legs were useless, feeling as if she had been ill for weeks. She crawled downstairs, raked out the ashes and lit the fire. She heated a tin of soup. It put warmth back into her.

The mare.

Who had bought the mare?

The thought nagged at her.

She couldn't sleep. She saw the mare, dressed in her Mayday finery, parading endlessly in front of stony faces; she saw the old man's eyes.

She woke next morning feeling ravenously hungry, cooked herself bacon and eggs and went out to the phone box. The post had brought her week's money. She rang the sale room.

'Who bought that Shire mare?'

'The knacker.'

Ned Knacker.

She knew him; had known him all her life. He came for the dead animals and he often brought her chocolate when she was small. He liked children; he took the babies to see his horses. He bred Fell ponies and showed them. She often stood at the field gate watching the foals. He was wary of her now she was grown—he was always uneasy with women, not knowing what to say to them at all.

But how could she buy the mare? Ned would want more than he paid for her, and she had no money at all. If she sold one of the cows, gave him an I.O.U. till the calves were born, sold the sow. . . .

She ought to be working in the cottage, it was a terrible mess. But the mare dominated every thought; Ned couldn't put that shining bravery down. She couldn't go for dog meat . . . it was a horrible thought.

If only he hadn't killed her already. It was two days since the sale. If only she hadn't had flu. She didn't know where the old man lived. She had to look up Ned's number. She rang, but there was no reply. She had to get there.

She had to look round the yard and the fields and see if the mare were there. She was going to buy the mare even if it meant offering to work for Ned, clean his house, do his horses . . . anything.

She would have the mare and breed the foal and if it were a filly foal she'd have two mares. There was money in Shire horses. She would breed them; would show her father that she could manage on her own. That he was wrong about her.

Quite suddenly the past few years seemed unimportant and trivial; years of growing up, not knowing what she wanted to do, what she wanted to be or who she was. Years in which her grandfather's genes had been crying out to her to acknowledge them, to acknowledge that she belonged with horses. If only she knew more about them.

If only Ned hadn't killed the mare.

She waited at the end of the lane, willing a car to pass, hoping for a lift. People gave lifts more easily in the country. There was only a bus every two hours, but she could come home on the bus. She didn't like hitching.

The car that drew up was driven by a woman.

'Please, are you going near Fowler Street?'

'I pass the end of it,' the woman said. They chatted about the weather and the price of food and the difficulty of buying good bread; the driver baked her own. Kate thought she might try. It would save money.

When she was straight in the cottage.

If she were ever straight in the cottage.

Fowler Street was a long miserable street of boarded-up shops and broken-down terraced houses. It gave way to an open field and to Ned's yard. A horse looked at her over the broken down stable door. Ned came out of his caravan.

'That Shire mare . . . is she dead yet?'

'I haven't even got her yet,' Ned said. 'Old Joe wanted to keep her for his last few days.'

'Why is he selling?' Kate asked.

'Got to leave the farm. Too old, poor old devil. They're putting him into the Home. Be the end of him, losing that mare. And she ought to have been sold to a good buyer; I'm trying to hunt one up for him. Can't put down a mare in foal. She should have been advertised. Joe was daft, but he's not making much sense, poor old gaffer. I bought her to try and do the old man a favour—he can't understand. He doesn't listen when I talk—he's in a fog and I can't reach through.'

'I want to buy her.'

Kate did want to buy her, more than she wanted anything else on earth.

'Ned, come into partnership with me; there's money in Shires. Good money—I'll look after her, keep her, and feed her.' I don't know how, she thought, but she'd do it. She'd make money, coin money, do anything legal to earn money. She had to have that mare. She was crazy, but Ned recognised the passion.

'Why didn't anyone else go for her?'

'She was put into the sale late. Word hadn't got round and there are no Shire breeders near,' Ned said. 'Look, go and see old Joe. Make him an offer, and see what happens. I reckon he'd give her to you to keep her alive. He dotes on that mare.'

Ned didn't add that if no buyer came forward the old man would shoot her himself, might have shot her already for all he knew, and not rung him yet. He liked old Joe. Known him for long enough, been over for his animals. He gave Kate the address.

'I'll run you over,' Ned said. 'Need to see old Joe myself.'

The old Land Rover rattled along the road. Kate sat silent, thinking about the Shire. She was crazy, out of her mind, not knowing how to pay for the mare. Her mother? That wasn't fair. She had to stand on her own now. She could have saved it out of her wages if she'd tried. Money thrown away on clothes she didn't need, on cosmetics she no longer wanted, on meals that weren't worth what she paid.

She'd had no sense of value, no appreciation of the way other people lived, having to manage as best they could on almost nothing. The money she'd spent on her hair each week would buy the cat food for four weeks; the money she'd wasted, buying clothes and petrol, buying things she didn't really need or even really want, would keep her for a year. She could have bought the mare several times over if she'd only saved, as her Mother had suggested only too frequently, when Kate had spent all her wages and needed to borrow. Life had been too easy, too much fun, never for real. She suddenly saw her father's viewpoint; he worked, he slaved, he devoted himself to the farm, to the animals. As she would have to devote herself if she were to prove her worth.

The days stretched before her, filled with chores. Cattle to tend and pigs to feed and muck out; and she would have to sit up all night if a sow farrowed unless she chose to be clever and do it by day. Suppose something went wrong and she needed a vet; how much were vet bills? Her father had always complained; she had never bothered to listen.

Suppose she did get the mare and the foaling went wrong, suppose the mare were ill. She had to have money; she had to earn money; she had to coin money. She had to find a way to supplement what her father gave her.

Defeat blackened her mood. Ned sensed it, but did not know why. He'd never married; women took too much time, and nagged a man. Both his brothers had married managing wives who had tried to manage him. Sam and Harry were much older; they'd endured homes that were neat as new pins, never put anything down for a moment without it being tucked away; come home on time, had their wage packets taken off them and money given them for beer and tobacco. Wouldn't do for him.

He'd never been wild, but he needed to be free; to come and go as he chose, loving the dark nights, out on the moors, walking, looking up at the sky and the moon, watching the beasts, not for killing, but because their lives fascinated him, out on the hills, wild and free; living in their own worlds.

He knew where the fox hunted; where the badger cubs played; where the otter whistled on summer nights. He could not read very well, he could not write very well, but other men knew less than he about the secret creatures that haunted the fields and rivers. He could rise when he chose, and fish before the day was bright; no woman to chide him. He could spend his money as he chose.

He never regretted the lack of a wife.

He drew up at the gate of Joe's farm. Kate looked at it, the shabby buildings and tidy, well-swept yard. Not even in his last week there, would Joe neglect it. The old man was standing at the field gate, watching the Queen as she grazed. He turned as they approached them.

'Not today,' he said to Ned.

'I'd like your mare, only . . .' it was the girl who reminded him of Ellie. Ellie as she had been just before she died. He could not bear to look at her hair. He wanted to reach out and touch it, as he'd touched his daughter's hair, wanting to tell her he loved her but never knowing how.

'She's no money,' Ned said. Better not hide the truth or give the old man hope. 'She's fields and to spare, but no money.'

'You'd give her a home?'

There was eagerness in his voice.

'I want to breed horses,' Kate said.

'She's old Simon Malone's granddaughter,' Ned said.

'Simon Malone, and you want to breed horses.' There was a light in his eyes. 'I don't want money for her. I'll give Ned back what he paid the auctioneer. He won't destroy a mare in foal. You can have her, look after her, just let me see her sometimes. Just to know she's alive, that the foal will be born . . .' he was tumbling over his words, wanting passionately to interest Kate, while Kate, as passionate, was seeing a prayer answered, a dream come true, knowing that there were too many snags; the need for money being a major need. She couldn't afford the mare. She'd cost money to keep. Be realistic, a voice said inside her head but she didn't care about common sense. All her life had been geared to this day, to buying her first horse, to showing her father what she could do. She was Simon Malone's granddaughter. His had been a famous name, all his life; as judge, as breeder, as exhibitor. She would do the same and here was her foundation mare.

She'd find a way of keeping her; of making money, somehow. There must be things she could do. If she rented the grazing; if she let out her fields; if she took in a lodger . . . but she needed a stable, and the thought rose unbidden of the derelict shack, tumbling down, that had to be repaired.

'I haven't a proper stable. . . .'

'I've time,' Joe said, eagerness in his voice. 'All day, every day, nothing to do. They'll let me out . . .' he made it sound like a jail sentence. 'I can still hold a hammer; between us . . .'

'She's still yours,' Kate said. 'I don't know nearly enough about horses . . . about anything.'

Joe held out his hand.

'Farmer's handshake on it,' he said. The fear of days spent pointlessly, uselessly, thinking of his past life and of his dead Queen, were banished; he could come daily on the bus to Hangman's Lane. He knew Willow Cottage. It was only five stops away from the Home.

Ned watched them, without any regrets at all.

They were both crazy; an old man, too old to work, and a girl with no experience whatever.

He drove away.

They didn't even see him go. Joe led the way indoors, where the fire blazed brightly, and there was point in bringing out the tea tray. He only had shop biscuits; nothing to offer her to seal a pact, but it didn't matter.

The fire blazed and there were dreams for both of them in the dancing flames.

Outside the Queen stood under the big oak, unaware that she had been given life, and that, only minutes before, her owner had been cleaning his gun, knowing that tomorrow, unless a miracle occurred, life would end for her and with it all his hopes.

'If we could show that foal . . .'

There was no way either of them could spare the money, but it didn't matter. Kate looked through the press cuttings books, where the Queens looked out at her from photographs. The May Queen and the March Queen; The Queen's Treasure, the Queen's Pride, the Queen's Beauty; and outside stood the January Queen, with a future in front of her again.

It was time to go. Time to return to the cottage and clean and paint and cook, and tidy. Time to return to reality. The mare would be over in the morning. Ned would bring them over. Of that Joe was sure.

Kate took the bus home. She was aware that there was very little in her purse, and that she needed so much for the cottage. She would have to learn to make do. She needed furniture. She needed to repair the stable; she needed to make the fields work for her. Money. Why did it have to matter so much? She could live on dandelions and nettles, on mushrooms and on berries, when the season came, but just now nothing was growing and she had to eat to live. Cold reality made her shiver. The cat was waiting at the cottage door, mewing with hunger. The kittens would soon be weaned and need food too. Kate cut brown bread and crumbled it into milk and fed the cat. She made herself toast and topped it with a small tin of beans, an egg added, and grated cheese. The clock she had found on the mantelpiece kept stopping. She needed a clock. To mark the hours, to plan a routine, to time the chores, to find time and more time.

She went to bed and dreamed of the January Queen, standing in her fields. But try as she would, she could never come near the mare. As Kate moved, the mare moved, and then a hedge grew between them, higher and higher, reaching to the sky, darkening everything. She woke and stared at the moon, dreading sleep. Outside an owl called and footsteps sounded on the path. She was alone, and she was afraid. The footsteps went round the corner of the cottage. Then there was silence. She crept to the window, wondering if the lock of the door would hold against an intruder. She had never felt so alone.

Moonlight flooded the overgrown orchard. There, under the tree, a pony cropped the grass, having wandered in. She went down and shut the gate. In the morning, she would have to find the owner. And afford it or not, she was going to buy a dog. She felt too isolated.

## CHAPTER TEN

◗◆◆◆◆◆◆◆◗

It was odd in the house without Kate. Nell had never had so much time. She couldn't believe Kate had accounted for all the extra work, but, when she sat down to consider it over her morning coffee, early in May, she realised that in fact, Kate had.

Her room always took three times as long to clean as any other room in the house. Clothes were strewn around and never folded; Nell could grumble, could plead, could cajole, but it made no difference. Make-up was spilled on the dressing table and often on the floor. Clothes to pick up, take down and wash, clothes to put away.

The bathroom was as bad. Wet towels on the floor; the floor also wet; rings round the bath; nylons in the washbasin, as Kate never had more than one pair unladdered at a time and usually found they needed a wash half an hour before she required them. Or she borrowed Nell's and ruined them.

Scatter-headed, addle-pated—that was Kate.

Even so it left a gap. Her room looked bleak and so did Tim's. He came home so rarely, stayed so short a time, filling the house with excitement. He never walked anywhere, he always ran, startling even Meg, who was used to more sober-minded men round her. None of the farm men moved fast; they walked slowly, careful always not to alarm the animals. Tim had forgotten about living with animals. He was full of plans, of news of his doings, breezing in, greeting them, settling like a butterfly on a flower and then he was away, impatient to find life again. Time stood still on the farm. Nothing changed.

Charles was too busy in his office. She rarely saw him in the evenings. He spent his time working out the accounts, brooding over details, trying to compensate for the money he had lost on the ram, sitting contemplating the wall, wondering how to raise funds for another ram from Amby. He wanted the new young one; Amby had better rams than he, all the time.

If only the ram hadn't died; but it was no use dwelling on that, nor was it any use worrying about Kate. Nell had driven over and found the house transformed and Bill had delivered the cattle and the hens, the sow, the ducks and the geese. A builder was working on the place, repairing windows and roof, and Kate was decorating the interior.

Nell, sitting alone watching the television set posture its absurdities, found herself wishing she was back again with the family at home. It was too quiet in the kitchen with Charles so busy, but he wouldn't give up. He worried at the figures, trying to make them more favourable, but they never would add up to the fortune he needed. Lambing was almost over, so at least they could rest at night.

One evening she sat watching Arthur Negus talking about furniture. She was half asleep, unusually exhausted, and feeling slightly unwell, for no reason that she could think. She started into attention when he walked over to a little desk that was, she was sure, almost identical with the one that her father had left her in his will. The old man had always said it was valuable, but she could not believe it could be worth much until Arthur idly quoted a price beyond her imagining.

If she could sell the desk she might be able to get rid of the old furniture, give Charles some decent office furniture, buy new curtains and chair covers, or even new chairs, and make up for the bleak feeling that had settled on her since Kate left home.

93

She was old. So old, and she felt even older when she went shopping for a new coat and the girl in the shop, younger even than Kate, chewing gum, with little interest in anything except her commission, had been unable to hide her contempt when Nell found herself in love with a frivolous garment the assistant obviously considered far too young for her customer; a scarlet coat with a hood and a dramatic fur lining.

The girl had looked across Nell at the other assistant and rolled her eyes. Nell intercepted the glance and changed her mind, walking out without buying anything. She went into a flowershop and spent a small fortune on flowers. Life had passed her by. She had no goal to achieve, no future to look forward to, nothing to do but mark time. Nothing more would happen to her now. One day she might be a grandmother, but that would make her feel even older. She was old enough to be a grandmother now. The thought stopped her in her tracks in the middle of the High Street and she caught sight of herself in a shop window—a dowdy dowager in a drab coat. It was a horrifying vision. Where had she gone to, during all those years? This wasn't Nell Malone, this old lady, with her tired face.

She walked to the car park, her feet dragging, her legs aching. She didn't want to go home. She wanted to be young again, to drive into the hills, to run against the wind, to pick snowdrops and primroses and come back and fill the place with flowers. Not this house, but another house, one which she had chosen, with furnishings she had chosen, not those that she had inherited; solid respectable sensible family stuff. She wanted to buy modern furniture; she wanted to be slim again and young again and she wanted to laugh again.

No one laughed in the house now that Kate was gone. They were all too busy, all too solemn. Rob had kept them laughing with his clowning and his jokes and she missed him, unexpectedly, and wondered where he had gone and what he was doing. He might have been good for Kate, but they were both young and it was a passing fancy at an age when you fell in and out of love with a boy as easily as you fell in and out of love with a new fashion, discarding your boyfriends with little more regret than you discarded your mini or your tatty fringed jeans or your peasant blouse. She had been beautiful at Kate's age. She had forgotten.

Men no longer turned to look at her as she passed. She was old, old and unremarkable. Their faces came alive when Kate was with her. Kate was vivid, vital, walking with a swing and a verve that attracted the eye.

Standing in the gloomy hall, holding the bright flowers against her, Nell felt forlornness sweep over her, and utter loneliness. No one was left to her. Charles would not notice if she were away for a weekend, a week, a month, if she walked out and left him for ever.

The house was sterile, pointless, a monument to a past that meant absolutely nothing to her at that moment. She looked about her. No one called; Charles's visitors went to the office where they smoked and laughed and drank his home-made beer. They wouldn't dream of doing that in here. Women were not really part of their lives. Most farmers were awkward except with their own wives, and on their best behaviour with her.

She was filling her life with pointless activities, hiding from herself how little she had to do that was necessary or worth while. Looking after the furniture filled the hours; but it was a sham, a pretence, and if she polished only once a year instead of almost daily, it would make no odds.

What was she doing here? She was an alien among aliens. Her family had grown away from her. Or she from them. She didn't know. Once she had turned when Charles came into the room, run to him, eager and expectant, asking so much from life. Life hadn't been like that.

Tomorrow and tomorrow and tomorrow creeps on its petty pace from day to day. And what was that song Kate was always playing on her record player. You don't bring me flowers any more. She bought her own now. Charles had no time for flowers, and it wouldn't occur to him she'd love a bunch from him.

They had flowers in the garden and she'd enough

money to buy what she wanted. What more could she want, he'd ask, if she told him.

She put down the flowers, her feet dragging. She knew why she had wanted the coat. It was to cover fear.

Fear of loneliness.

Fear of old age.

Fear of the lump she had found the day before in her breast, a tiny lump, barely more than a pinhead.

A warning of much worse to come?

She didn't know.

She walked into the kitchen and began to put the flowers into vases, but she couldn't see them for the shine in her eyes. Bill, coming to borrow a pair of scissors, looked at her, and sensed her distress.

'What's to do, lass?' he asked.

It was more than Nell could bear. The man had been with them for most of their farming life, and was almost part of the family.

Bill said nothing more, and made tea. Death and birth, misery and despair, happiness as well, you made tea. Daft, he thought, as he filled the pot.

Nell had always been able to talk to Bill. She had sat with him at his wife's bedside, the long nights when Mary lay dying, Nell's presence a comfort to both of them. Her old nursing skill had returned and she had been useful and needed; had almost enjoyed her rôle. Now she wished she hadn't been a nurse. She knew too much; had seen too much in those long years in the wards, during the war, before she married Charles.

'I'm down, is all.' Nell said. 'I found a lump . . . and I've terrified myself.'

'Seen the doctor?' Bill asked.

'I'm scared,' Nell drank the tea. It was far too hot, but dear God, she needed it. Needed comfort, and cherishing and being wanted. Needed to wake up and find she was dreaming and the wretched thing wasn't there.

'I'll make an appointment.' Bill believed in knowing the worst at once. You could face it then. It was the unknown fears that were always those that overset you. He went to the phone in the kitchen. There were extensions all over the house.

'Don't tell Charles. Not yet. It's probably nothing.'

'Probably,' Bill agreed, 'but it's better to know.'

Nell was only half listening. She had been gripped by a wave of utter terror that reduced her to unreason. They could do so much now, but . . .

'Tonight at six-fifteen. I'll drive you over. If you come down to the house, Gaffer won't know. You can say you're going to a meeting. He'll be busy. The Accountant's coming. I'm going off tomorrow to try and find a dog. We need another dog. A good 'un.'

'I'll give it to Charles for his birthday.'

Bill looked at her and followed his own line of thought.

'They don't stay babies for ever,' he said, knowing the gap in his own life when his two daughters left home. He pottered around the house now like a single pea rattling in a pod, and talked to the cat for company. They came back, but it wasn't often. He preferred to be with Charles—two middle-aged men in the office, talking cattle and sheep until exhaustion set in and you knew that sleep would come fast.

Then he went home, across the yard, stopping to look at the calves and hoping maybe a cow would need him and keep him with her so that he hadn't to face the house where nobody moved any more except himself and the cat, and she was getting old too.

'You have to find a new way of living,' Bill said, 'do something different.'

'Like having a breast off,' Nell said, and then wished she hadn't. She didn't know what made her say it.

Bill went out of the room.

He came back five minutes later with two slices of iced cake. Nell stared at it.

'I made myself a birthday cake; iced it and put ten candles on,' Bill said. 'Like dressing for dinner in the jungle. You don't give up.' He grinned at her. 'Maybe a sign of second childhood. I just fancied a birthday cake. Long time since anyone even knew when it was my birthday.'

Nell thought of the red coat. A coat for Kate, not for her. A longing to go back? She didn't know.

A few hours later she faced nightmare, as the doctor looked at her.

'A good job you came early,' he said. 'Into hospital as soon as I can get you a bed; tomorrow if possible. You'll see the specialist in the morning. And you know as well as I do it may be nothing.'

'And it could be malignant,' Nell said. She didn't want to face that.

'It probably isn't. Stop worrying, Nell.' They had known one another a long time; worked together in the operating theatre long ago during the war; gone their own ways, almost forgetting each other until Martin put his plate up when their old doctor died and they met one day in his surgery, when Tim had crushed a finger, playing where he shouldn't. There were too many hazards on a farm.

The next night and day were a nightmare. Bill drove her to the specialist. There was a bed free. She went home for her case, packing it in a dream. Charles had gone to market and she had said nothing. Bill would have to tell him when he got home.

She lay in the white bed, terror riding her. She tried to read. Bill had gone out and bought an armload of magazines. They would operate tomorrow. By tomorrow night . . .

She didn't want to think about it.

She wondered what Charles would say.

She woke as he came into the room, roses spilling from his hands. He must have combed the shops for them. She stared at him.

'You idiot, Nell. Why didn't you say?'

She couldn't say anything. He sat by her, holding her hand, sharing with her a future that might be unthinkable.

# CHAPTER ELEVEN

◆◆◆◆◆◆◆◆◀

Nell woke muzzily. A nurse was standing by her bed, smiling at her. She felt sleepy and relaxed, aware of pain, but not much pain. Slowly, remembrance returned.

'It was a tiny fatty cyst, nothing that mattered at all,' the nurse said. 'So you can go to sleep and when you wake up again, your husband will be here to help you celebrate.'

It seemed an absurd thing to celebrate. Nell lay, half dreaming. She had faced terror. Imagined herself dead and buried and her life wasted. When she came home she would make changes; big changes. She had to get fit quickly. There was so much she wanted to do.

Charles came into the room, and walked over to the bed. He stood there, towering above her, looking down.

'You hopeless idiot,' he said again. 'Why didn't you say?'

'I only discovered it that day,' Nell said, 'and when do we ever have time to talk?'

Charles sat beside her, talking farm talk, which was the only talk he knew. Maribelle had a bull calf; Hanibull had a sore hock; the ram lambs were soon to be sold.

'I want a red coat with a fur lining,' Nell said. She couldn't get it out of her head.

'Why on earth don't you buy it?' Charles asked, puzzled by her tone.

'Mutton dressed up as lamb,' Nell said.

'That's crazy. You look good in red. Buy it when you come out; a get well present from me.'

It was lunatic, but she'd do it, if it were still in the shop.

She suddenly felt like a teenager again, dreaming of a wonderful dress for a party.

She had insisted neither Tim or Kate were told unless there was anything seriously wrong. She was so short a time in hospital that, a week later, the whole episode seemed like a dream.

She had never looked at the landscape round the farm before. She saw it suddenly with a painter's eyes, the light behind the trees, the swelling buds on the willows. Once she had wanted to paint. Long ago. She had painted moderately well, but she hadn't touched a brush in years. She went indoors. She'd drive to town and buy painting things; and she'd buy the red coat. She needed different occupation; a new lease of life had been given her and it wouldn't be wasted. She went into Kate's room and rummaged in the wardrobe, among the clothes she had left behind. An old pair of faded jeans; a thick jersey, hooded and warm; a green duffle coat. Green wellington boots. She changed and stared at herself.

She was still slim, almost as slim as Kate. She'd lost weight recently. With a scarf to hide her hair she was a different person. No one would recognise her. She thought of the committees she sat on; respected, elderly, dressed in sensible dignified middle-aged clothes. A frump. She'd resign from them all. They were only a gap filler. She'd start painting, re-furnish the house, buy Charles a dog; she'd been given her life back again, nothing altered, but she'd been through hell and come out safe and everything was upside down.

Yea, though I walk in the valley of the shadow of death. . . .

She couldn't remember how it went on.

She went downstairs and out to her car. She'd sell it and buy something different; it was too big, too solemn, an absurd vehicle for one woman. It reflected a middle-aged image. To hell with images. Bill, seeing her, stared, and then grinned.

Nell had had a shake-up all right and it had had the right effect. Thrown everything she knew into the melting-pot, made her re-assess her values; and by the look of it she'd come up with an answer. He wondered where she was going in such a hurry. It had shaken Charles too.

Nell had an objective and she wanted to reach it before she changed her mind. Halfway to the town she drove the car into a layby and looked at the hills. Snow lay unseasonably on the tops, glistening under a slanting sun that threw the shadows into deep relief. The new budding trees reflected the light as if lit themselves from within; the world was being new made and she had never noticed spring before; had never had time to look; had always been hurrying somewhere, an objective in mind. Butter. Jam. Sugar. Tea. Meat for the freezer. Epsom salts and toothpaste. What a way to spend a life.

She stared at the hills and the cloud patterns and the shadows; at the budding trees and the bright primrose-starred banks, yellow stars scattered liberally over the green. A white head looked at her over the fence; a bull calf, his eyes shining at her, his nose working, his ears moving, alive with spring and youth and enthusiasm, unaware of his own future, content with now.

She wanted to put him on paper; to put the hills on canvas, to paint the sudden stirring excitement that coloured everything around her. Why hadn't she noticed before? She had been obsessed with household chores. Shapes and patterns were here, flung with a random splendour that no human could emulate. The rich curves of the hills, the sweep of hedges, the white buds just awake, the line and fold of the valley, the contours of the peaks beyond, stretching away to a blue haze that hid shape and dwarfed humanity. She was a tiny entity, of no more importance than the inquisitive bull calf watching her through the gate, and she had thought herself important, wasted years building up a personality that was totally false to her. It had been a long time since she had laughed. Taking life seriously and herself too seriously. And the family too seriously. Maybe taking the world too seriously. It wasn't much of a world; a tiny place of one's own was the only possible peace. Outside it was chaos.

101

She had lost incentive. She had never changed her ideas. She wanted time to paint again; time to walk on the hills, time to relax. She'd re-make Kate's room into a studio; it had a good North window, a huge window, looking out on to the fields and hills. She might have another thirty years to make a new life; years in which grandchildren could be born and grown up and married, and here she was feeling time was short. Thirty more years and she couldn't live it like this, day after day the same, with nothing to look forward to.

Charles had the beasts and the planning of his herds and the new rams and the new cattle and the possible show wins; she had emptiness, arranging endless flowers that died on her and were thrown out and new ones picked. Endless meals to make and clear away, endless nights at the end of endless days, when she had nothing to put in her day book, if she ever kept one, but 'got up, made breakfast, cleaned the house, went shopping, made lunch, cleared away, did flowers, made tea, sewed, made supper, went to bed.'

She'd remodel the garden—create a huge bank of alpines, turn over the back lawn and increase the orchard. She could make wine; her father used to make wine. His gorse wine had been special, something to taste and linger over and try to make again next year, and his rose petal wine had been superb.

She let in the clutch, checked the mirror and drove out on to the road. She drove to Seton, the biggest town, twenty miles away. She lunched quickly and cheaply in the Green Man, a beef sandwich and a shandy. The landlord was interested in boxing; pictures of sparring boxers were hung behind the bar, pieces cut out from newspapers, a signed photograph proudly displayed, a pair of boxing gloves hanging beside the new warming pan on the fake brick wall.

She found the art shop and bought brushes and paints extravagantly, eager to go out and try her hand again. It would not be easy. She found two books on drawing and one on water colours; another on painting in oils. She bought a canvas and stretchers. She'd go home and try her hand at painting a flower. She'd plan the new orchard. Apples and pears, peaches and plums, damsons and raspberries, gooseberries and black and redcurrants. She could grow masses of strawberries, and maybe start a business of her own. She needed, so much, to achieve. And she had, as yet, nothing to show for all those years of living except two children who had grown up and were now adults, having to learn how to live alone. They did not need her.

She pushed the thought out of her head, and drove home again, unpacking the car as eagerly as a bride unpacks a trousseau. She had forgotten to leave food for the men. Charles had been in and found the cold joint she had cooked the day before. The remains of the meal was on the kitchen table. The floor was muddy. Three weeks ago she would have set to work to put it to rights, resenting the work they made.

Now she looked at the mud and promptly forgot it, and went to Kate's old room. She rolled back the rugs, and set up her easel.

Her work was infuriatingly amateur, a daub. She needed to learn, to learn so much. She looked at the painting with distaste, as Charles came into the room.

'Where on earth's supper?'

'I forgot. I was painting,' Nell said.

He stared at her.

'Have you gone mad?' He was startled when she laughed at him.

'No, Charles, I think after all these years I've gone sane.' She wiped her brushes and put the caps back on the tubes of paint. 'I'm cold. We'll picnic by the fire.'

Charles looked at his wife. There was red paint on her chin. He did not remember the jersey she was wearing; it was sky blue, something that Kate might have chosen, but never Nell, who always dressed with such discretion that he could not even remember what colours she wore. It suited her.

He went outside, to stand and stare at a promise of a moon, hanging over the five barred gate as if some child had cut it out and suspended it there in the sky. The fields were hidden in darkness, but the reassuring sounds of

many beasts came to his ears. The heavy breathing of con-
tented cattle, the odd bleat and baa of a sheep and lamb,
the rustle from the calf pens, where the calves spent the
night on straw. They were good sturdy little beasts this
year, not one ailing, and he was proud of them.

He resisted the temptation to go and look at them. They
were bedded for the night. Meg came out to stand beside
him. He wondered if dogs ever speculated about the moon
and stars. The light from Nell's window shone over the
yard. He stood at the gate. It was an evening ritual; his
own reward for a day well spent. The animals grazed in
the fields. It was the end of winter; buds opening on the
trees; a promise of future harvest. He was worried about
Kate. He didn't like the thought of her on her own; yet it
was high time she did leave home.

He thought about Nell. Her days in hospital had made
him realise how lonely he would be without her. They saw
little of one another, but she was a vital part of the household—the mainspring. Without her he'd be totally lost.
Maybe she'd like a dog of her own. . . .

It was supper time, but there was no sign of Nell.
Charles was glad she'd found a new interest; rushing
around on committees seemed a waste of time. He avoided
committees; avoided meetings unless they affected the
farm and his work, though he liked the evenings in the
Plough—the talk of sheep and cattle.

Too much time to think tonight. The light was off in
Nell's room. He hadn't wanted to interrupt her; she was
enjoying herself with her painting, and he was delighted.
They'd both had one hell of a shock; and it had done nothing but good in the end.

She came across the yard. There was a spring in her
walk that hadn't been there for years, an eagerness in the
way she moved. As if suddenly she had found a purpose.

'I spent too long painting. I've no energy to cook,' she
said. 'You don't mind, Charles? I've made sandwiches to
eat by the fire.'

'I always did like sandwiches,' Charles said. 'Like old
times, when we were first married. There was never time

for anything else—you had the babies and I had the stock.' He followed her indoors.

'We had Tim too soon,' Nell said. 'Ten months on our own and never time for one another since. Never time for anything.'

She poured coffee into two mugs. Bright blue mugs, one labelled HIS and one labelled HERS.

'Kate gave them to us for Christmas. I hid them away, I thought they were horrible,' Nell said. 'But tonight's a new night. I'm going to paint again . . . though perhaps I've left it too long. I always wanted to get back to it, but I never had time, or energy, or . . .' she hesitated. She had been going to say the need, but maybe it was better not said.

'Grandma Moses was eighty, or was it ninety?' Charles said. 'It's never too late.'

'I didn't even know you'd heard of Grandma Moses,' Nell said. It was years since they'd talked about anything except passing the salt and there wasn't any cattle feed and had the knacker phoned.

'I saw an exhibition of hers once, in a thunderstorm in London.' Charles laughed. He'd been on his way to Smithfield when the downpour began. Taxis had vanished like snow in summer, and he'd gone for shelter and then been fascinated by a vibrant primitive innocence that was like nothing he had ever seen before.

'It would be nice to have grandchildren,' Nell said, changing her mind about being old. Charles stared at her. He never could follow the jumps in her thoughts, but the idea had been triggered by the phrase Grandma Moses. She'd like to share her painting with grandchildren. She had always been too busy to share with the children. Maybe she'd failed Kate and Tim; not listened to them enough, her mind on the next job, on the need to make meals for the men. She had always had at least ten to feed, with her own family, and sometimes more. Charles fed his men as an extra to their wages; it helped to keep them.

He put more wood on the fire. The flames glowed and leaped, bringing warmth to the room. A fire made a house into a home; there was something institution-like without that background in the hearth. He took a sandwich and looked at Nell. She was gazing into the flames, seeing pictures, analysing colour and shape, thinking of scenes she could put on canvas. She looked different and then he realised her hair was cut in a straight close cap, and that she was looking at him with Kate's face and Kate's eyes. She had lost a lot of weight.

'I like your hair,' he said.

'I didn't think you'd notice.'

'I notice.' Her clothes were different too. Cream slacks and a blue bloused shirt caught in at the waist and throat, and a padded waistcoat. She looked half her years.

'I'd like to alter the house,' Nell said, 'sell off the old furniture. That desk might be worth a lot of money now. I'd like simpler things; I want space and air all of a sudden. I don't know why we kept that heavy old stuff.'

'We never had time to think about anything else,' Charles said, stretching long legs to the blaze, avoiding the dog at his feet.

'We can start with your study, make it comfortable. It's intimidating as it is. It would be fun to start again. I almost envy Kate. I wonder how's she getting on.'

'Bill says Kate's a survivor. I wish Tim would write or ring more often. I'd like to know what he's up to.' Outside in the byre a cow lowed persistently. 'Lulu's started calving, and it's high time I went to make sure she's OK.' Charles levered himself to his feet. 'I suspect we need Vic. She had trouble last time.'

He was gone, and Nell lifted the phone and dialled, to warn the vet that he might be needed later on, and then found a cookery book and browsed through the recipes, trying to plan meals that would take less time to prepare and be as nourishing, wanting time for herself; time to paint; time to hunt new furniture; time to re-plan the house.

Just for the two of them, with a guest wing for Kate and Tim when they came home. She picked up the photograph album and turned the pages. Tim and Kate as babies, at school, as teenagers. Kate in her first dress, in her confirmation outfit, as bridesmaid at a cousin's wedding. Tim staring at the camera, his expression brooding, enigmatic.

She went out into the yard where light spilled on the patched cobbles.

'We're in trouble,' Charles said, coming out to meet her. 'Can you ring for Vic? Can't manage on our own.'

Nell went in and dialled quickly. Her message given, she stood at the window, the cow's bellows a constant background to her thoughts. Poor Lulu. She was having it tough but with luck the calf would be there by morning and take her mind off her present terrors. Nell saw patterns in the night. She teased them in her mind, wanting to put them down on canvas, and went up to the new studio, forgetting time, as soon as she saw Vic arrive.

She painted the shadows in the yard, the light and the darkness alternating; she wanted an air of brooding, an air of waiting, and she painted Meg in, Meg as she always sat, watching for Charles to emerge so that she could take up her life again.

Charles, coming in, stared at the empty bed. Was Nell ill? He ran down to the little sitting room, and then up the stairs and saw the light in the studio. He went in, expecting to see a watercolour or a flower picture.

What he saw startled him. The dog, head cocked, listening. Nell had captured her, perfectly. There was the yard, the patched shadows, the open cowshed door, and an air of waiting. Meg never left him when she was fit. There was more to it—a feeling of hidden buildings, of action somewhere out of sight. He couldn't pinpoint it, but realised some minutes later that it all stemmed from the dog, ears pricked, listening.

Nell had it all: the expectancy, the atmosphere, the mystery of night.

'By God, that's good,' he said.

'It's better than I expected. It isn't right.' Nell looked at it critically. She didn't know what it lacked. Something. It needed more time, more thought, more feeling. She hadn't given it enough time. She hadn't lost her skill. It needed to be brought back to life, but it was still there.

Excitement mastered her. She could paint. She could paint. She could paint. It was a litany to sing while she sought sleep.

## CHAPTER TWELVE
◆◆◆◆◆◆◆◆◀

Joe was making plans again. The mare need not die. Elation filled him. He looked at Ellie's photograph for a long time, wondering if she could have reached out to him, have sent Kate to the Beast Sale that day, had touched Kate with the need for the mare. He didn't know.

He didn't care.

He walked outside with the bucket and stood watching the Queen. It was no longer the last time. It was a new beginning. He could sleep in the Home, but he could spend the days helping Kate, if she'd let him. Time with his mare.

Time to see the foal born.

He was an old man, but if God were good he'd a few years left in him yet and work in his hands, though he was no longer as hale as he had been. And his memory played absurd tricks. He still thought of Ellie as being twenty; this girl could be her daughter.

He would have to work out his finances. The auctioneer had been to the farmhouse and looked at his furniture. Joe had seen scorn in the man's eyes. A young man, a brash man. They were all brash, the young men, and had lost politeness over the years, discussing him as senile, an idiotic old has-been.

'Won't fetch much. It's old, but not old enough,' he'd said scathingly and Joe had hated him; hated his tanned face and neat little black moustache and his brown eyes that priced everything, even the frame on Ellie's picture.

He felt the contempt for age, as the man stood, considering curtains and the worn carpet, the new rag rug that Joe had pegged himself last winter, liking the occupation. The old armchair.

'You'd do as well giving it away,' the man had said, and had written down the date of collection. Wednesday week. That night he would hand over the keys, would be gone. The Queen would be with Kate at Willow Cottage and he'd be sharing a room with another old man; he'd not shared a room since his wife died and he didn't want to now.

He wanted to end his days as he had lived them—his own man. Choosing when he slept and when he ate, out in the early morning, milking his cattle. The farm was empty without them. The fields looked empty too, and someone else would cut the barley this year. It was new growing, young, and looked like a good crop. He'd always done his best.

He wished My Lady hadn't been in Australia; she might have influenced them, just for one more year. They respected her, though maybe if she wasn't My Lady they wouldn't listen to her. She wasn't due back for another month. She had the wanderlust, that one. He liked her. A man could be straight with her, tell her when she was wrong—and she listened.

He could maybe keep the old Land Rover. He rarely used it. There was life in it yet. It gobbled diesel. Maybe Kate would have somewhere to house it, and she could use it if she needed transport. But he had to be careful; she might resent him, might not want him around; might want the mare and the foal but not the mare's owner. She might have just been kind, but she had the necessary passion. He'd seen it in her face. He stood, uncertain, the keys in his hand.

He could go over and see, couldn't he? No harm in that. He had new-baked scones and bread; he had a new lease of life, and laughter in him as the Queen's wise head leaned over the gate, a question in her eyes.

'I'll be back,' he told her. He always told her that. She didn't understand but she liked the sound of his voice. He looked at her, waiting for the engine to stutter into life—always tricky starting. She was the most beautiful mare he'd ever had.

And she was going to live. Joe had been unable to realise that Ned would not put the mare down. Misery had prevented understanding.

He hadn't lost the feeling of elation. He swung out of the gateway and down the lane, through the open gate that never needed closing now as the cattle had gone, and out onto the main road. A four mile drive to Willow Cottage where Kate was busy sweeping out the dilapidated stable.

She smiled as she saw Joe. Anything to break the loneliness. She had never been lonely before. There had always been someone around to talk to. Now, she had only the cat in the house and the kittens.

'It will never be fit for a Queen,' she said, making a small forlorn joke, despair in her voice.

'Needs a bit of tidying, is all,' Joe said briskly, recognising her misery.

'I could do with a coffee,' Kate said, and led the way inside.

The house was a home now, walls white-washed, shelves painted, and the room bright with curtains and cushions Nell had made, and furnished with pieces from her old home.

'I'll bring the mare as soon as we've fixed the stable,' Joe said. 'I'd like to help with her, only I don't want to be in the way.'

'Would you come over and help?' Kate couldn't believe it; someone who really knew about horses, here daily, to help her learn. She wished she had known her grandfather for longer. He was a wizard with horses. 'I don't know anything about horses really, and I'm scared stiff I might do harm through not knowing.'

The coffee was a toast to a future, a pact between them. Joe felt young again, ready to tackle any job. There was so

110

much to do here, so much needing doing. Gates to mend and walls to repair and fences to see to. And all on such a small scale; nothing like his farm that ate into his time and took more energy than he had.

'We'll fix the stable up a treat between us,' Joe said.

He took the broom and went out to finish sweeping the stable while Kate made lunch for the two of them. She took it out to the orchard: coffee and sandwiches, and Joe's scones, buttered and jammed, melting in the mouth. The stable floor was clean now and they could see what needed doing.

Charles had had the cottage repaired, but the builder was too busy to start on the outbuildings and Kate had not told her father she needed the stable. She intended to show him she could manage alone.

'We'll have that fixed for the Queen in no time,' Joe said.

He knew he was being optimistic, but he wanted to cheer them both up. He looked at the cottage before he drove away, and saw in it a promise of days of occupation for himself; a far call from the dreary time he had expected to spend, sitting waiting to die, knowing that the Queen was dead, and that all his life's work had been wasted.

The drive home was quick, the roads almost without traffic. He went into his farmhouse and began to sort out his treasures. This for Kate and that for the sale room. The new rag rug would look bright and gay in her little sitting room, and she could have the china horses that stood on the shelves. He'd take just his silver Shire to the Home; nothing else. The bits and pieces he wanted were already there in the little attic that would be his home now for the rest of his life.

He could dig the garden and they'd grow vegetables for the summer and that would save money. Potatoes and lettuce; peas and beans; beetroot and spinach and broccoli. Kate had four cows; they'd have milk and butter and cream and cheeses; and there was going to be a sow, about to farrow; they'd have bacon. And pork. A goat in the orchard to keep down the grass. The money from his furniture would help.

And his hens; he went out to look at the dozen he had kept till last, intending to kill them for the table. They were all laying. One of the sheds would convert to a henhouse and he could put up a run. Use this wire; it wasn't part of the farm; or was it? He was unsure, but at least the hens didn't go with the rest of it. So Kate would have eggs, and maybe enough to sell. They could run a little farm shop, put a notice in the Post Office window. He was full of plans. He'd saved nothing over the years. There was nothing to save for after his wife died.

## CHAPTER THIRTEEN

◆◆◆◆◆◆◆◆

'They're crazy,' the man said in the Plough, hearing the gossip—the story of a girl of twenty and a man of eighty in an absurd partnership based on a thirty acre smallholding and one brood mare that had been bought by the knacker, and then somehow, handed back.

There were others who embroidered the story, but luckily neither Joe nor Kate heard those. They were both finding a new meaning to life.

The cottage was now a home; cleaned and painted, outside and in. Lucky and her kittens lived on the rag rug, made, they were sure, for them. Joe's chair was still Joe's chair—old, the hide scratched by generations of cats, the filling coming out of one cushion, held in by Kate's first attempt at a cushion cover. It was there by the fire for him at coffee time, and when he had a cup of tea after his lunch, needing to sit and regain his energy before starting on yet another job around the place. He couldn't bear to part with the old chair. He'd sat in it for nearly sixty years.

At night he went back to the Home, but Kate fed him first. He hoarded his money, a use for money at last. Money to buy Kate lengths of new curtain material for the kitchen/living room; money to buy her a model of a Shire horse to put on the mantelshelf; money to use to show her that he appreciated being in partnership with her; money that would have been used for the daughter Ellie had never lived to have.

Joe might have been Simon Malone; he thought the way her grandfather had thought; his talk was of horses. Always of horses.

His first thought when he came in the morning was for the Queen. Kate watched him come in through the gate, in the old Land Rover he had decided not to sell. It was useful transport for both of them; to fetch hay, to bring him in the morning; to go together and buy the week's groceries—Joe, always canny, with a Scottish mother who had trained him well, watching the prices, teaching Kate without her even knowing she was learning.

Hay for the Queen had to be sweet; had to be fresh; no hint of mould or mildew, not a trace of fustiness. He held it to her nose.

'Smell that, it's not good enough.'

He was angry when she made a mistake. She had to be right. Had to learn fast. He hadn't enough time.

Kate learned to use her nose. She knew the smell of a healthy mare; the clean smell of the Queen as she came to be petted. She was used to being talked to and fussed. Her first days in the field had been uneasy, but once she learned that Joe came always, soon after nine o'clock, with the titbits she loved, she relaxed. Kate brought her titbits too, and soon Kate was greeted with the welcoming whinny and the quick thunder of hooves as the mare cantered towards the gate and braked, putting her head down for a caress.

Joe cajoled her, telling her how much they wanted the foal.

He brought out the pedigrees and showed them to Kate.

He pointed out the horses that had gone into making this foal one of the best foals in the history of the breed. At first Kate laughed, and then, as she learned more, she realised that Joe knew exactly what he was doing; that this foal could be one of the best foals ever bred.

'I kept her breeding dark,' Joe said. 'I didn't want her to go to some get-rich-quick merchant, out for a high price for her and her baby. That's why no one bid for her. I would rather see her dead than in bad hands.'

She was all the family he had had for the last few years. That and his old dog. Butch had died six months before and he hadn't replaced him. It wasn't easy to start a new pup at eighty. He might die when the dog was still a puppy and what would happen to it then.

But he hated life without a dog, and Kate was on her own at night and he knew where he could get a nice pup. They bred them at Brayshaw's. Nice little Labradors, intended for working, not for the show ring. He'd no time for Breed showing in dogs; it ruined their working capabilities, as tomfool women and some men went for colour, for shape, for the set of an ear, and the lie of bones that nature never meant to work in that way. A dog needed brains and legs that moved; and a tail that wagged and a life that was a life, not a life led between kennel and show ring.

He did not tell Kate of his intention.

'I'll be late next Monday,' he said, 'got some business to do first.'

'Will you be here for lunch?' Kate asked. She hated eating by herself.

'Should be.'

They were working on a second pigsty.

Charles had offered his daughter one of the older sows, about to produce her second litter. There had been no problems with the first. He did not want Kate to have the worry of a first-time farrowing.

Nell drove over, taking with her a week's baking. She stood at the gate, looking at the cottage. Kate had been slaving; there was little sign of the slum it had been when she took over. The new curtains were bright in the win-

114

dows. The kitchen/living room was a friendly place, the fire in the grate casting shadows in the corner. Lucky and her kittens purred in front of it. The fire no longer smoked. The sweep had cleaned the chimney.

Joe's pictures hung on the wall. A race-horse; four Shire horses; a matched pair ploughing a long field; one of his champions, standing regal in his show bravery, the man beside him holding a silver cup.

'Mother!'

She hadn't seen Kate come in. Kate dressed in jeans and work jersey, her hair tied back in a pony tail, her face, without make-up, glowing with excitement.

'I hoped you'd come. Come and see it now.' She led Nell round the place; into the bedrooms, now white painted, and curtained; one in a pattern of tiny blue flowers, the other in a cream and fawn trellis of honeysuckle. Matching spreads that had come from Joe were on the two beds. His rugs were on the floor which Kate had smoothed and stained, Joe showing her how to use his electric gadgets to good effect.

Joe had brought her towels and sheets and pillowcases and table linen, from his own store. She repaid him by feeding him. Outside he had made a start on a kitchen garden, having bought a little secondhand rotovator. The Queen was standing against the hedge.

'It looks lovely,' Nell said. Kate realised her mother looked different. Her hair was cut short, fringed, and she wore scarlet trousers and a white jacket. Nell had rarely worn trousers when Kate had lived on the farm.

'You look fantastic. Have you lost weight?' Kate couldn't pinpoint the difference.

'Lost weight, had a re-tread, and found a new occupation,' Nell said. 'I've never had time before.'

Or energy, she thought, recognising now that constant work for the family had drained all her enthusiasm and initiative. She had been occupied with surviving as best she could.

'What are you doing?' Kate poured water into two mugs containing instant coffee, and opened the cake tin.

'Dropped scones—fantastic! I need your recipe. Mine won't come up like this.'

'You can have your grandmother's cookery book,' Nell said, 'I know it by heart. I'm painting again, going to classes; and I sold your grandfather's little desk. The price I got was unbelievable. It will refurnish the whole house.' And two more, she thought, but she didn't say so. She had still not recovered from the shock. She had never realised how much genuine pieces would fetch in the modern market. Charles had stared at the cheque when she showed it to him.

'My God. I don't believe it,' he had said in his turn.

'I'll buy you a herd of top quality cattle and a new ram,' Nell said, 'and twenty-seven sheepdogs.' She had been feeling light-headed.

'I'll settle for one.' They had laughed together. Bill had found a new pup that was now part of the household.

They named it Cub, because it looked so like a wolfcub, with its fuzzy puppy fur and absurd little endearing face. It would be very heavy coated when it grew, unlike Meg. And it adored Nell, following her around hopefully, bringing her presents of pieces of wood, or an odd potato that had fallen from a sack and landed in the yard, or a chicken feather. She was never sure what would be offered to her next.

'We've a new pup, she's called Cub,' Nell said. It was time to go home—the pup was not yet reliable in the house, and she was in the kitchen, where she had a basket under the table. Also she chewed; Nell was not used to small pups and their ways. It was more than four years since Meg was small. The wastepaper basket had been emptied the night before, the paper torn into minute pulpy shreds, lying all over the kitchen.

Cub could jump onto a chair and then onto the table and steal the food. She had knocked over a case of flowers and strewn the flowers around the floor. Anything might happen in Nell's absence.

'Tim's rushing round the country as usual,' Nell said, as she was leaving.

116

'Tell him to come and see me when he's next home—then I can show him my farm,' Kate said, and laughed.

Nell was anxious to get home. It was absurd to worry about the pup, but she did. Suppose Cub got into the cupboard under the sink where the disinfectants were stored, and the dishwasher powder. Was it shut tight? Nell wasn't sure.

'Come again,' Kate said. 'I'll give you lunch.'

She watched her mother drive away and went out to the sty, where Joe was busy hammering. Tomorrow was Monday, and he wanted to make up for the time he would miss.

He was looking forward to bringing a pup to Kate. He had already inspected the litter and chosen her dog—a Yellow Labrador. The parents were both there; it wouldn't be too big. They were sweet-tempered, all of the dogs. He'd made very sure of that. It was the most important part of a pet dog. He'd seen some swine in the show ring, but you could hide that, while the judge looked. You couldn't hide it on the bench and you couldn't hide it from those in the know. And he knew his dogs as well as he knew his horses. You got it in all breeds, some vice. In Spaniels and in Labradors, in German Shepherds and in Cairns; no breed was perfect and never would be. But if the breeder knew his job . . .

He drew up at Brayshaw's.

Ted Holloway met him. They were Ted's dogs. He lived in a cottage on the farm, and had turned the garden behind it into one big kennel complex. It was superbly built and everywhere was spotless. Ted cleaned up whenever he saw the need, and the girl that worked for him took immense pride in her work. She adored the puppies.

Joe looked about him.

Brayshaws were famous for their stock. Their foals fetched high prices in the auction ring, if they ever got that far. He could put his finger on a number of names in the racing news, all bred from here. The winner of last year's Derby, the winner of the Oaks two years ago, and the mother of another Derby winner had come from here.

117

They were elegant horses, unreal to Joe, who preferred his massive beauty. She'd make two of any one of these.

'This is our pride and hope,' Ted said, as a chestnut mare put her head over the white post and rail fence, and nuzzled against him. 'She's a sweetie, our Conker. Her foal's due in about seven months' time.'

'Same time as the Queen's,' Joe said. But a very different cup of tea. The Queen might fetch a couple of thousand pounds in a sale, if those in the know were there. This mare was worth a king's ransom.

'She's insured for a hundred thousand pounds, and the foal the same,' Ted said, guessing his thoughts. He hoped to see more of Joe. They both talked horse, and though they bred different types, the basics were the same and Joe had an eye for a horse. He's been watching the mare for some minutes, not hearing a word that Ted said.

Mick Brayshaw came towards them. He was a lean man, a man with dark hair and dark eyes that gave him an almost Spanish look, stemming from an Irish grandmother who in her turn had been descended from a man wrecked in the Armada. The dark good looks skipped a few generations and then came back. Mick was only half Irish but he had inherited the horse-mad half.

'She's our major achievement, and all our ambition,' Mick said. He put a hand on the soft neck and the mare turned towards him, whinnying softly. She slept in a stable next to the house; she wandered loose around the yard when the gates were closed and it was empty of traffic; she put her head in through the kitchen window, to be stroked and talked to and given titbits. She loved fresh baked bread, and stole the loaves if they were put on the draining board to cool. She was everyone's pet and she knew it.

She was Mick's main reason for living. His marriage had lasted only two years. His wife had gone skiing with her parents in Switzerland and died in an avalanche. That was eight years in the past. Eight years during which he had dedicated himself totally to his horses, going nowhere. Ted had tried to persuade him to take a break but he would not leave the farm, except to do business.

A friend of his mother's had become his housekeeper

when her husband died and she found herself badly off. It was an excellent arrangement for both of them. Louise Grey had her own flat at the top of the house, and her own furniture; and she too loved horses and was always ready to help if a girl or a lad were ill.

'You foal's due at the same time as mine,' Joe said.

'So we may both find ourselves with fantastic winners; or total losers,' Mick said. 'I picked a splendid stallion, but you never know.'

'Could mean good breeding in two generations' time from the foal,' Joe said. He had memories of foals that had been sure-fire winners, and had grown into also-ran horses. Breeding was a mug's game when you thought about it, but while the foal grew inside the mare, you hoped and you dreamed and you planned for its future—the foal of all time; the champion at every show; the father or the mother of champions; the horse men would talk about and write about in years to come and say, 'That was a horse'.

He'd never bred it yet, but he'd come near and so had Mick.

Time was running on and he was dreaming and Kate needed him back there to finish the sty and improve the stable and mend the byres; an in-milk cow would make a difference; every penny counted for both of them.

'I'd better take that pup,' he said.

Ted led the way to the kennels. There were only five of the litter of eight left. The other three had already gone to their new homes. The pup he had picked was wearing a little red collar round its neck, with his name written on the white tab in felt-tipped pen. He watched it wrestling with its brother. It was going to be lonesome tonight.

He had the cheque already written.

'I don't want Kate to know the price,' he said. 'She needs a dog, down there alone at night.'

'It's a spooky place, Hangman's Lane.' Ted hated it for some reason he could never explain. He had been riding a horse across the fields when it had shied at nothing and tossed him in the ditch. It had refused to move, and he had had to return the way he came. That, they told him, was where the old gallows stood. He didn't believe in spooks; he didn't believe in atmosphere and he knew his feeling was all nonsense. All the same, he wouldn't have lived up that end of the lane for a thousand pounds.

Joe knew how he felt. He had walked in the lane only a few nights before and seen movement where no movement ought to be. There was nobody and nothing there, but the feeling persisted. He hadn't mentioned it to Kate.

He picked up the pup, which fussed against him, trying to chew his hand, wagging its absurd tail, delighted to be singled out for attention. He had left the Land Rover in the lane. He went down the drive, and stopped to look at the mare. She was beautiful; one of the most beautiful animals he had ever seen, her lines not yet hidden by the growing foal. She came to him, sure of her welcome, treading delicately on legs that seemed absurd when he compared her with his Queen. They looked as if they'd break at every step.

He had pony nuts in his pocket and held out his hand. She took them daintily and dipped her head to his shoulder and rubbed against him. She nosed the pup and the pup licked the velvety muzzle, quite unafraid of this enormous creature, secure in the man's strong arms.

Joe whistled as he drove back to Willow Cottage.

Kate was making lunch when he walked into the kitchen. She smiled, and said 'Hi', and then stared at the pup in his arms.

'He's yours,' Joe said.

And five minutes later rushed outside with the blazing frying-pan, that Kate had totally forgotten.

The incident sobered both of them.

Kate made sandwiches and brought out Nell's scones and cakes, and they ate in the garden, watching the pup, now anchored by a long piece of clothes line, as he busily explored his new territory.

Joe went out to the sty and brought in four pieces of linked fence wire, nailed onto a wooden frame, carefully hinged.

'There's your play-pen, pup,' he said, and took off the line and dumped the pup inside the barricade. 'You can take it indoors,' he added to Kate. 'It'll save a lot of worry with him. He's safe as houses in there. No chewing flexes or getting hot pans poured over him.'

Kate, trying to clean the burnt pan, was unable to concentrate. The pup, now in the kitchen, his pen lined with sheets of newspaper, was busy in his own way. The paper was nice to tear, and Kate had given him a tin plate to play with, found in the garden shed and scrubbed until it looked almost new. It would make a plate for his meals, but right now it occupied him and he couldn't hurt it or himself. He crashed it round the pen. Kate filled a bowl with water.

The pup inspected it, tasted it, and tipped it over the floor. When she turned again he was sitting on the soaked paper, the bowl up-ended in his mouth, over his eyes, hiding his face, whining, as he tried to decide how on earth he could see again.

She rescued him and removed the paper, and took away the bowl.

Time had never flown so fast.

And she was only just beginning to realise how much she didn't know about animals—horses and dogs alike.

She put down a hand and he nibbled at her finger. He was hungry and Joe hadn't given her a diet sheet. Joe remembered, and came in with a bowl of milk and puppy food, which Ted had provided. They both stood and watched the pup eat as if he had never seen food before in his life. He licked the plate, and then began to hunt for a place to squat.

Joe grabbed him.

'Out at once after he's fed,' he said and the two of them went out to watch the pup perform, and then Joe praised him as if he'd just given them the Crown Jewels.

'It's the only way to tell him,' Joe said.

The puppy wagged his tail. He'd done right and it was a good feeling.

'If there's anything you want to know and I'm not here, ask Ted,' Joe said, as he prepared to go back to the Home for the night. 'He's the sort of chap that keeps tabs on his dogs, but doesn't interfere; and he's always glad to help with any worries. He said just come up; he's usually there and if he isn't the kennel girl is. And their horses are worth seeing too. It's a beautiful place.'

There was a touch of wistfulness in Joe's voice. If he'd had the money he'd have had his own breeding farm; not one mare but twenty, and then he could have made a real mark in the Shire world.

He left Kate and went to say goodnight to the Queen. She looked even more massive after the mare at Brayshaw's.

They were both planning for the future; they were all dreaming dreams. You could with livestock. You never knew what would come. It could be wonderful, it could be disaster, but it was always interesting. Tomorrow he'd finish the sty. They'd get the sow, and there'd be little pigs squealing out there. Kate would need all the help he could give. He was useful again. No one would guess he was eighty years old. He felt as spry as he had at sixty.

He whistled as he drove, thinking of the future and two mares in the field, and both of them in foal. Kate would make her mark on the Shires, they'd make a fortune together. He turned in at the drive and was instantly deflated. He hated the place, and he hated the attic room that he shared with old Mr. Perkins, who had a hacking cough and snored wheezily and talked constantly of his ailments, most of which were in unmentionable places, but the old man wasn't deterred by that. Never mind.

There was always tomorrow and Kate's little farm to tend; and it was fun teaching her. He lay awake for a long time, listening to his room mate snoring and thinking of Ellie. The thought no longer hurt.

# CHAPTER FOURTEEN

◖◆◆◆◆◆◆◆◖

Joe came daily. At first he had been diffident, afraid that Kate might not want him around, but she greeted him with such delight that he soon knew he was welcome. There was too much to do; both of them were fully occupied, day in, day out, and soon they had formed their own routine.

Kate milked the cow, now part of her stock. Joe had made the byre habitable. There was a new small bathroom, attached to the kitchen, and hot and cold water, so recent that it was a luxury.

Nell had chosen a new cooker. It wasn't fair to leave Kate with something so old that it was dangerous. She and Kate had spent a day together going round the showrooms, inspecting, assessing, looking for reliability and Kate had ended with a self-cleaning oven that was a godsend.

She didn't know where the time went.

It went on teaching the pup his manners. She'd named him Tearer, as he spent most of his time reducing the paper that lined his pen to confetti. He greeted her with wagging tail and wagging body whenever she appeared, almost oversetting the pen in his excitement.

He made all the difference.

At night, when Joe had gone and the curtains were drawn and Hangman's Lane was locked out, she had the cat and her kittens and the pup to amuse her. Tearer came out of his pen and explored busily, finding a brush to carry, or her slipper to bring to her and drop into her lap, or he and the kittens chased through the furniture, sliding on the rugs, always busy, always interested. Life to all of them, was total excitement.

The pup was intelligent and easily trained. Soon he was lying at her feet, not needing his pen, coming when she called him, always eager to greet her again, even though he had only left her a few minutes before. He knew the meaning of No, which was a big advantage. His parents were both working dogs. It made a difference, Joe said. Show dogs often had no brains at all and their pups had pea brains.

The mare took time. Time to feed her. Time to water her. Time to groom her, to get the caked mud off her feathers, to keep her in tip top condition, to ensure she was used to being handled. There might be problems with the foal. Time to greet her, to stroke the big wise head, to smooth the soft mane, to give her her favourite titbits. Joe walked her daily, doing both of them good. Those driving down the lane grew used to the sight of the old man and the big black mare, walking in all weathers.

The sow was now in her sty, with eleven baby pigs around her. Kate brooded over them, worrying. Were they getting enough milk from their mother? Were they all healthy? Suppose they died on her? One little pig did die: a ne'er do well, Joe said, examining it. Too small at birth and not able to hold its own, no problem.

Suppose he were wrong and it was the start of swine fever? Or foot and mouth? Or some awful disease she had never even heard of?

She had never imagined she could feel so anxious about baby pigs, but these were her pigs; money in her pocket in future and she needed money.

She had never realised how much money it took just to survive.

Joe was planting vegetables which would lessen that bill; even one apple cost six or seven pence, and she'd been used to eating two apples a day at home, not even thinking, not to mention a pear or so and oranges and bananas.

And meat was a total luxury. Joe taught her to buy belly pork and breast of lamb, to stuff a sheep's heart, to eat tripe and onions and to spin liver out with streaky bacon. She learned to make thick lentil soup that was satisfyingly hot after a morning working, and dumplings to go with it. She learned to make an apple fool that was mostly custard and cream from her cow. She learned to make interesting meals from potatoes and fried onions, with one chopped tomato and grated cheese.

The pigs fed on potato peelings, on the waste from the Home, which Joe had asked for and which came daily. Kate boiled it all well, and fed it thankfully. It saved her pounds on extras. There were always left overs; the cooks at the Home were far from brilliant.

The mare was showing visibly now, aware of the foal, knowing that soon she would have a baby to care for. She waited, watching for Kate and Joe to break the monotony, enjoying the pup who, now he was allowed more freedom, came daily to visit her. Tearer was sure the mare needed his company. He inspected her field, marching in front of her, a small, muscular, determined little beast with a welcoming grin on his face as he turned to make sure she was following him.

'Give him a leading rein and he'll walk her on his own,' Joe said one morning, watching the Queen plod after the pup, as if they had decided on an outing together. Often on a fine day he stayed with her, and if she dropped to the ground to rest, he curled up against her, delighted to have company while everyone else was too busy for him.

Willow Cottage was now home. Kate loved it—her own place, her first home, and though it had been her idea of hell to start with, she now revelled in it.

Joe had begun to laugh again, enjoying a new sort of life. The Home was bearable as long as he was fit and could come down daily to Kate's and help with the beasts. He was teaching her, and neither of them knew it. Rob was a fading memory but she did not want to be hurt again. She avoided involvement. Joe's talk was of Shires and of Shire breeders, men he had known, men whose horses he had judged. Horses he had coveted. Horses from the stud book that he had seen and remembered from long ago: Eaton Premier King, Kirkland Black Friar, Lymm

Coming King, His Excellency, King Mountain, Herontye Buscot, Golden Farmer, Harold's Rival—names that stuck because they were famous; names that stuck because they were odd, like Gunby Autumn Tints, or Calwich Bridegroom; names that stuck because he had judged them.

'Now, there was a colt,' he'd say, opening up a bale of hay for the Queen, struck by a sudden memory. 'Black, seventeen hands, with two white socks; sweet tempered as they come. I can see him now, though his name's gone and his breeder's name with it, at Windsor in 1927. . . . '

The memory drifted away. He could no longer remember names well, yet sometimes, from the far away past, came complete scenes, unbidden, more vivid than yesterday.

Kate had never enjoyed life so much. Sometimes Joe stayed on for an evening meal and Ted Holloway came over, at first pretending he wanted news of the dog, but later admitting his life was lonely. Mick Brayshaw had little time for social affairs—he was completely wrapped in his horses, and had been to the exclusion of everything else, ever since his wife had died.

Kate was fascinated by Ted's descriptions of Eleanor Brayshaw. She had been beautiful; and had loved skiing more than anything else in the world, always going over to Switzerland with her parents for the winter sports.

The avalanche had killed fifteen people, her father among them.

Mick went nowhere now. Except, rarely, to market, or to negotiate for a horse. His buyers always came to him. It sounded a very lonely life. Kate, dishing up meals that Joe had taught her how to prepare, learning to make one penny do the work of five, listened to the two men talking. Ted was half Cockney, quick to laugh, quick to mock; Joe enjoyed a joke but was more solemn. To both, horses were a passion, almost a religion.

At times they would argue amiably on the virtues of the Shires as against the racehorses, but it was never serious; merely a leg pull. The meal ended, the two men always washed the dishes while Kate locked up chickens, put the cows in the byre, and went out to see to the pigs. The little ones were soon being weaned and their squeals at feeding time often drowned all conversation. They were active, lively, and extremely mischievous. They were running free by day in a part of the field that Joe had fenced off with an electric wire. Tearer had soon learned that electric wires meant a tingling nose, and he kept well away. It hadn't occurred to him that he could jump over them.

Spring turned to summer without Kate even having time to notice. Joe had planted beans and peas, spinach and beetroot; and had suggested he buy a deep freeze which would fit into the little outhouse that backed on the other side of the kitchen. Kate could pay him back over the weeks. There was going to be so much garden produce and he would benefit from it too. They would go and select it in a week's time.

It was almost mid-July. Joe, looking out over the fields, had a sudden shivery feeling. Things were going too well. Something would go wrong—with the Queen? With the pigs? There was trouble in the wind. He'd always had a nose for trouble. He'd known there would be disaster the week that Ellie died. He hadn't known what. He'd known when his wife was dying; long before even the doctors believed that she could not live. He hated the feelings of trouble ahead, but he'd always been right. Kate wondered at his sombre mood. He went back to the Home early. He had a feeling that trouble was waiting for him there.

He knew as soon as he saw the official-looking envelope, neatly typed, the postmark unfamiliar. It was the bill from the syndicate for dilapidations on his farm. One thousand one hundred and twenty two pounds and sixty seven pence. How on earth did they arrive at sixty seven pence, he wondered, wildly, not wanting to take in the significance of the figures.

He had very little in the way of savings. The sale of his furniture had realised only a few hundred pounds; he'd had nothing of value. The farm had taken every penny he had, to run it well. There had never been much profit. He had made ends meet, had a few pounds for emergencies in the bank and prided himself that he had never had an overdraft; he had never thought of having to pay for things he had neglected during his tenancy.

He looked down the list.

The rotten fencing in the fifteen acre field.

The guttering on the house, was that his affair? Surely it was My Lady's—and wasn't she responsible for dilapidations, not him?

He couldn't face supper.

Matron came up to see if he were ill, having seen him come in and found him sitting on his bed, staring at the wall, looking as if he had received a death sentence.

He assured her he was well, but had had bad news; and she left him to contemplate a future that had changed again, dramatically, within minutes of his homecoming. He had only one asset in the world.

The January Queen.

Find the right buyer and he could get a thousand pounds easily. He would have got more at the auction if he hadn't put her in in a hurry and had no time to advertise her. He hadn't put a reserve on her. He hadn't really wanted her sold.

No deep freeze for Kate. And if the Queen were gone, both of them would have lost their future. They'd been living in a fool's dream; an old man and a girl, with no mind for reality. He should have known, should have remembered; every tenant farmer knew about dilapidations. The syndicate were business men. They wouldn't let him off. Would My Lady lend it to him? He couldn't ask her.

How did a man make a thousand pounds, when he owned nothing and was unable to offer his labour to any farmer because of his age? As a young man he could have worked and saved every single penny, living rough and feeding on bread and cheese. Now he could earn nothing. He went to bed and lay for a long time staring at the wall. There were no solutions.

Life had been good and now he was pitchforked back into misery again. Man was born to sorrow as the sparks fly upwards; or was it trouble? Maybe he should have gone to church, have been a better man, have placated a God that he neither understood or felt sure about; maybe he should have poured libations to other gods, to Fates and Furies that seemed more real than the Christ figure the churches offered.

It was a very long time before he slept, and every wheeze and groan and snore from the old man in the other bed was an irritation he found almost unbearable.

He knew, by morning, what he had to do.

He called on Kate to tell her he was spending the day in town, and made a list of errands. He would be back by the evening meal. Could she manage alone?

She would be busy, but she could manage. She watched him drive away, worry niggling. He had been subdued and almost morose, a faraway look in his eyes. She wondered if he felt ill and was about to see a specialist, and had not wanted to worry her. She missed him more than she had believed possible. He had come for part of every day; never intending to stay, always a little afraid he might be unwanted, an old man hanging on to life when he should be letting go.

Kate valued him. He knew what to do when things went wrong, even if he could not manage to repair them himself. He was there when the sow farrowed. It was his hands that brought away the last little pig, coming into the world hindfirst and not headfirst; easing her with the sow's contractions, gently, gently, never harming either of them.

It was he who showed her how to gentle the Queen; taught her the horseman's liturgy, the soft repeated 'Easy girl, easy there, whoa there, easy there, come on girl then, good girl then', over and over the voice soothing, reassuring, no movement made in a hurry; and the grooming sssssssss that kept the dust out of nose and mouth, and the mare silent, watching the man, her ears moving to catch the sounds. Now Kate's voice was as welcome to her as Joe's, and when Kate came down in the morning, very early, to fit in the day's tasks before darkness made it impossible to work, the mare greeted her with that quick pounding gallop to the gate and a high excited whinny of welcome.

Kate couldn't bear to be without the mare. She wished she had had the money to buy her from Joe. If she sold the weaners; and two of the cows, both in calf; if she spent the evenings knitting and sold her produce from the hens; if she learned to dressmake; if she filled every hour of every day, there still wouldn't be enough to pay a fair price.

Joe helped her for nothing, telling her that the mare's keep and the field she was in were worth more than his labour.

If her grandfather had lived she would have gone to his farm as soon as she was grown and worked with the horses. But Grandfather had died and the horses had been sold. Working with the Queen brought back memories; Joe was so like her grandfather. Maybe all horsemen were alike.

She filled the bucket with water over and over again before the trough in the field was filled. That was Joe's job. She had not realised how heavy the bucket was when it was full. Too heavy for an old man. She broke a bale of hay and sniffed it. Sweet and pure.

She took it to the Queen in the wheelbarrow and tossed it over the gate. It was her morning treat; and after that was a feed of Joe's Special, which he had made up for all his foaling mares.

It was a grey day, heavy with clouds that were filled with rain. It would rain later. She cleaned the stable; the Queen would have to spend her time indoors if the weather fulfilled its promise. Kate had not realised that Joe had taught her to read the sky.

She knew when wind was due, and knew the fine weather and the foul weather sunsets. 'Bad day tomorrow,' Joe would say, looking at the horizon. The fields rose to the sky on the other side of the river.

The Queen's field flooded at times, but the water never lay deep or for long. She had learned to watch for the telltale signs: the first slow inching over the banks, which soon would spread, so that the water lay dark and sullen, reflecting the sky.

If Joe were ill . . .

She couldn't bear the thought.

It kept recurring all through the morning. He was old, so old. Her grandfather had died before he was seventy and so had her grandmother, and Joe was almost eighty-one. He had been alive before the turn of the century; had known a world she couldn't envisage, speaking of days when the fields teemed with rabbits and hares, and he and his brothers went out with a dog and a gun and brought home food for all the family; jugged hare was always on the menu. There were partridges on every ploughed field, nesting in the long grass, driven out when the corn was harvested; pheasants flew at almost every step from the hedges.

He would stop, while grooming the Queen, and say, unexpectedly:

'I remember when there were poppies in the corn.'

Red poppies. Now a poppy was a crime. How had the world changed so much? When had money become a God?

'It's all the computers and the accountants; we did very well without them,' Joe said, only the day before. 'Men had work and took pride in it. My uncle worked in a bank. He wrote figures that looked like little pictures, none of your unreadable modern scrawl. And banks didn't make mistakes in his day. Out by a penny and everyone stayed overtime to find it; now they can make mistakes of thousands of pounds and nobody cares. It's the computer.'

She made herself a quick sandwich. There was time for nothing else. If Joe had to give up, she'd never manage. She ought to bake the bread, but she had to clean the pigsty. The hen run needed cleaning and she hadn't collected the eggs. The pup needed worming, so she mixed his food and the worm pills and hoped he wouldn't notice they were there.

Tearer was too hungry to care. His food was overdue by half an hour, which he had spent crying in his pen for her to come and see to him. She needed to change the paper; he should have gone outside but she hadn't had time. And he couldn't come out with her yet, unsupervised, as he had a built-in suicide impulse. Only two days before, he had dug under the fence and slipped down the bank into the midden; he had been rescued, filthy and choking and it had taken all afternoon to clean him up. He had never smelt anything so exciting.

He wanted to get into the pigsty but the sow would never allow him near her babies. He knew that the wire round the field patch hurt, he had banged his nose on that. It was low, to keep the little pigs inside.

Why had she ever imagined she could farm on her own? Suppose something went wrong with the Queen? Was she eating properly? Kate went to look at the mare, and was greeted by a head that rubbed against her shoulder.

Time crept on, and yet the jobs were still half done. She would need to work out a rigid routine if Joe did have to rest. She couldn't afford help. No wonder her father had said she could never manage.

She would have to cut down somewhere, but she needed a cow for milk and another cow to get in calf, or she'd have a dry period; she needed the pigs to help with her own feeding and with her finances; she needed the hens for their eggs, and the chicks, and they could be killed for the table. And she needed the mare.

The Queen was her future; she would buy her from Joe as soon as she had the money. It was building up in the Bank, slowly, too slowly. She wished someone would call, perhaps would come and distract her; or Ted would come down to see Joe and talk horses, or the postman come by with a parcel, or someone call and ask the way. The time stretched endlessly. She talked to Tearer who wagged his tail. She had to stop to make herself tea. Her legs ached and her arms ached and her back ached; she had carried water and lugged hay; had cleaned an endless succession of stables and sties and henhouses—she had never realised how large they were. Joe usually did those. Guilt niggled. The work was far too heavy for him. She hadn't realised. Maybe he had dropped dead in town and would never come home at all. Maybe he had gone looking for somewhere else to live. She knew he hated the Home.

She went out to look at the old garage. There was a big room above it, that had been used as a store room. She climbed the rickety stairs. It had been used as a flat. She had never even bothered to explore before. The back of it

132

was filled with old furniture, total junk that needed to be burned, but beyond the big wardrobe that she heaved out of the way was a door. It led to a tiny bathroom, the bath old and rusty, the wash basin cracked. And on the other side behind an old dresser was a kitchen, with a sink and a stove and cupboards.

It would make a flat for Joe.

She went downstairs again into the rain. The Queen was standing at the gate. Her coat was already damp. Kate led her indoors, talking softly.

She dried off the damp coat. She tied on the nosebag. She patted the swelling sides. Only a few weeks to foaling time. Only a few weeks before they had a baby on the farm—and such a baby. Excitement mastered everything, even the fears for Joe.

They would clean up the garage flat; they would make a home for Joe, right here, so that he need not travel. He could be alone with his own things, with his books and his radio, which he never had a chance to hear now as everyone at the Home talked.

How they talked. Jabber, jabber, jabber, Joe said. He loved music, but he had no chance to listen to it except in the evenings with Kate when they settled down on either side of the fire, and Kate knitted and the soft sounds soothed both of them. They loved the same kind of music: the dreamy music of the ballet, the stirring Scottish songs that made toes tap and fingers dance.

Where was Joe?

It was past five and he'd been gone all day; suppose the Land Rover had crashed? He was getting too old to drive. She was tempted to run for Ted, but what could Ted do? Ring the police? She prepared the evening meal; everything Joe liked especially, hoping he would come. If only she were on the phone, but that was an expense far beyond her.

The cottage was lonely; sounds outside were magnified into noises that made her afraid. The wind cried in the trees; it would blow into a gale before night came. Wind slapped straw in the yard, slammed a door somewhere upstairs in the house, so that Tearer barked, again and again, and again and again Kate checked the yard. Was there someone there, hidden in the barn or the byre; was there someone trying to steal the Queen? She must get a padlock for the stable, because at least that would make a noise if it were broken, but how could she fight off a thief or thieves?

It was over a mile to Brayshaw's. She had never before felt quite so isolated. Suppose she fell and broke a leg? It was easy enough to slip on the cobbles. Suppose she needed help urgently when the Queen began to foal?

Joe was five miles away at night; Brayshaw's was nearer, but she'd have to run through the dark lane alone; she had no transport. Perhaps if Joe wouldn't take over the little flat he would at least let her drive him home and bring back his old Land Rover, so long as it didn't break down . . .

She baked potatoes; made a cheese sauce for the cauliflower; put two chops on to grill. They only had meat twice a week. She had Joe's refrigerator, which stored a certain amount of food. She peeled apples and made a custard; made an apple crumble; poured the cream from the top of the milk and went to milk Tossie, who had a habit of throwing her head in the air and kicking out at the bucket, which had earned her name. It was quiet in the byre; Tossie was in an amiable mood, and the sound of the milk flowing freely was soothing.

Outside the wind was blowing into anger, riding through the trees, shaking a loose board somewhere behind her, an irritating unceasing noise that added to her nerviness, making her wonder if someone unknown were hammering there.

It was almost seven when Joe drove into the yard behind the cottage. He had made a gateway so that the Land Rover could stand by the back door to be unloaded. He unloaded the hay. Kate, coming out of the barn, had never been so pleased to see him. He grinned at her, and humped out a huge box of groceries.

'We're celebrating,' he told her.

'Celebrating what?' Kate could think of no reason whatever for any celebration. It wasn't her birthday and it wasn't Joe's. His was five days after Christmas. Hers was in October.

'I'll tell you after we've eaten. I'm starving. Didn't have time for lunch.' He was excited, reminding her of a child about to go to a party, his eyes brilliant with suppressed eagerness. The table was laid and the food was ready.

Tearer went to his box. No begging at mealtimes. Joe was firm with his dogs and had shown Kate how to teach the puppy his manners. He was a bright little dog and soon learned what was expected of him. Joe made rules and stuck to them, so that the dog knew exactly what to do. Never on the chairs meant never, not sometimes yes. Never beg at table meant never, not sometimes yes. It made life easy for the dog.

Joe brought out a bottle of Mateus Rosé; Kate stared at it.

'Thought we'd make it a real celebration. My wife used to love this. We always had it on special occasions.' Joe was busy with the cork, pouring it into tumblers as Kate had no wine glasses, tasting it.

'I'm no judge of wine. Just like it now and again. I'm a beer person,' Joe said, and Kate laughed. Ned Knacker when he called was apt to say he was not a music person, or not a vegetable person; Joe mimicked him when he had gone. Ned dropped by at times to look at the mare. He was as fascinated by her as were Joe and Kate. He could have made a fair profit selling her, but he wouldn't have sold her to just anyone, not a live beast. He couldn't bear horses or other animals to be ill-treated.

The meal was good and Joe said so, always ready with praise. He stoked the fire. Kate drew the curtains and turned the radio on low. If Joe moved into the flat . . . only it needed so much doing to it. It was in worse shape than the cottage. If only she'd realised it was there. But it had never occurred to her to move the wardrobe and the dresser that masked the two doors. She wondered when it had last been occupied.

It was only a stone's throw from the house. Joe would be there when the mare foaled; would be there on hand in any crisis; and if he weren't well, she was nearby too.

'This is for you,' Joe said, and handed Kate a long envelope.

'For me?' She looked at it, bewildered.

'Open it, girl.' He couldn't wait. He watched her impatiently, willing her to hurry.

She opened it. It was a deed of gift, announcing that the January Queen belonged entirely to Kate Malone.

'Joe. You can't! She's your horse.'

'And what happens to her if anything happens to me and I haven't made everything plain? They'll sell her to add to my estate for my sons. It was either that or leaving her in my will, and I thought it was better this way. I'm no yearling, and if I have to go into hospital or if I die suddenly, I'll know she's in the right hands and where I want her.'

Kate had no words at all. She stared at Joe, and then went over and kissed him on the cheek.

'I don't know what to say,' she said.

'No need.' He sighed. 'I suppose I'd better get back to my room and old Snorer.'

'Joe. I found something today. Get the torch and come and see before you go.'

Kate had almost forgotten. The Queen was hers. The Queen was hers. It rang in her head, and she couldn't believe it. All the same, the Queen would still be Joe's. They belonged together, and when the old man went the mare would fret. It wasn't a thought to contemplate.

Outside, the wind was battling with the trees. Clouds flew across the face of the moon, making it look as if it were flying across the sky. Kate led the way up the steps.

'Go carefully, they're very rickety,' she said.

The torchlight flashed on the room over the garage. It was a big garage with a workshop bench at the rear, and this was a big room. The two doors stood open. Joe went forward carefully, exploring.

'Could we do it up as a home for you?' Kate asked. 'I hate it down here alone at night, it's spooky. It was worse than ever tonight. It's not in too bad a state of repair.'

'We'll do it up if it's the last thing we do,' Joe said. 'Just think of it, no more of old Snorer.'

'If you live here rent free it will make up for the mare—I just can't take her for nothing, Joe.' She was worth far more than Kate could ever hope to pay.

'We'll make a go of it, girl.'

He drove away, sounding the horn gaily as he went. He had just been to the doctor and been passed as fit to drive for another year. 'You're as hail as a man twenty years your junior and fitter than a lot of those,' the doctor had said.

He lay awake listening to old Snorer, and thought of the mare. Nobody could sell her now to pay for those dilapidations. She didn't belong to him.

He had taken the letter to his solicitor, who had executed the deed of gift for the mare; it just needed Kate's signature. They had considered the letter together. The solicitor was writing to the syndicate to suggest that as Joe had no means beyond his pension, most of which was taken by the Home, that he should pay down as much as he could and pay off the balance at five pounds a week.

If he moved into Kate's flat he would be fifteen pounds a week better off and would never miss the five pounds. And he had no fear of losing the Queen. He would be company for Kate, and it would be neighbourly to be near. There was so much he could do around the place still, although he did tire more quickly these days. Take it gently and he'd be fine. As strong as a mule, the doctor had said. He wouldn't have to drive five miles there and five miles back every day, that would save his energy. He and Kate could go into partnership—Makin and Malone. Horse breeders.

He grinned to himself in the dark and was glad that old Snorer couldn't read his thoughts. He'd think him daft as an onion and maybe at that he was. All the same, life had much more to offer than he had imagined only a few months before, when the syndicate told him he'd have to go.

It was a good thought and he fell asleep, though his roommate's snores blended with his dreams so that he woke once, sure he had heard a bull roaring, and then realised what had caused the images, and lay quietly laughing to himself.

Only a few weeks more and he'd have a home of his own again.

So snore away, old Snorer.

## CHAPTER FIFTEEN

Nell was halfway to Kate's cottage before she realised it was Saturday. It made little difference on a farm. It might make a difference to Kate. She hadn't seen her for two months; had no idea how she planned her week. She had taken nothing with her this time except a little painting of the farm to remind Kate of her childhood home.

Nell drew up at the gate, to find a party in progress. Ted had come over from Brayshaw's and brought two of the men; Joe was there and Kate was handing round coffee and sponge cake, a cake that Nell couldn't have bettered herself.

'We're making Joe a flat over the garage,' Kate said, as her mother came in. 'Did you know there was a flat up there?'

'I didn't even know there was a garage,' Nell said.

'Come and look.'

Kate couldn't wait to show her mother. They had cleaned out the old furniture, woodwormy and motheaten, and Ted had started a vast bonfire well away from the cottage. The two doors stood open, showing the little bathroom and the tiny kitchen.

'It's horrible in the Home,' Kate said. 'Joe shares a room with an old man who snores and there isn't any privacy. And it takes almost all his pension. He can help with the Queen when he lives here; he's given her to me, in case he dies suddenly, just to make sure she's in good hands. Look at her. Isn't she gorgeous?' She stood at the window looking down. The Queen was standing by the gate, watching the men work. She loved company.

Nell, using a painter's eye, realised the mare was gorgeous. The lines of the foal showed plainly—she would make a marvellous picture of imminent motherhood, and a pair to it could be painted when the foal was born.

Nell looked back at the flat; at the dirt on the floor, at the damp paper coming off the walls; at the grimy windows. There was a great deal of work to be done.

She imagined herself in a Home for old people, never alone. Joe would have his own place and he would be near to Kate. She hated the thought of Kate alone at night, even with the puppy. He wasn't as yet much use as a guard dog. Kate had to protect him, particularly from the onslaughts of the cock, which had been given to her by Ted as they had too many at Brayshaw's.

Monster was all cock and a confounded nuisance, chasing his hens constantly, crowing before the sun had deigned to open an eye, charging at the dog and at the goats. Occasionally he flew at Kate, and settled in the bucket of chicken food, helping himself as she carried it, scattering it with furiously scratching claws.

Nell, seeing him, wanted to paint him too. King of the farmyard, regal in his vivid colouring, his brilliant comb bright scarlet, his tail feathers peacock-hued, arrogance personified—if a cock could have a personality. It was the wrong word but nothing else would do.

'I've never known you daydream, mother,' Kate said, aware that her mother's thoughts were far away from her.

'I learned to do that in hospital,' Nell said, not thinking.

'When were you in hospital?'

'A few weeks ago.' No need to worry either Kate or Tim unnecessarily and no need to tell them at all, once she found it was a false scare.

'What was wrong?' Kate looked at her mother, appalled. 'Why on earth didn't you tell me? I'd have come home and looked after you.'

'I didn't need looking after. It was silly in the end, a tiny cyst, but it could have been worse. I'd have told you then. It wasn't worth bothering about. I was only in for three days.'

Kate did not know what to say. Suppose it had been really serious. It could have been. She didn't keep in touch with home, except at intervals, as there was so much to do. Her parents weren't young any more. People died in their fifties.

She walked over to her mother and hugged her hard.

'I'm glad it wasn't anything serious,' she said, 'but if you or Dad are ill, tell me. I want to know. I'd like to come home and look after you.'

'I'll tell you if we need you' Nell promised.

'We want to get the flat ready as fast as we can,' Kate said. 'Joe mustn't do too much though. He's very active, but he does get tired when he does too much heavy work. He won't be told.'

'Men never will. I'd like to help, Kate. It would be fun. It's years since I did any decorating; with several of us working on it, we could get it done within a week. The stripping down will be easy. This paper comes off if you look at it.' Nell pulled at a loose end and found herself almost swamped in damp paper.

Kate laughed.

'I did that, too. OK. We need furniture as well; maybe you could go to a sale or two for us; Joe doesn't mind what he has. He sold all his when he left his farm; of what was over after he'd helped me. He won't take back what he's given me. He says a gift is a gift and you don't have it back again, and he'd like a change anyway.'

'There's stacks of our stuff still at home,' Nell said. 'I haven't got rid of much of it yet.'

'We'd be glad of it,' Kate said, meaning it. It would save money.

'It will be fun to do this; let's make lists. But we must

140

ask Joe. He's going to live here.' Nell found a pen and a piece of paper and began to make notes.

Ted had ideas too, and some of his own furniture was surplus. He lived alone in a flat over the stables. Somehow, horses had never left him time to marry. They filled his life.

There was no room left over for anything else. He thought of nothing else, and his first contribution to Joe's new home was a picture of his favourite mare, a long ago beauty, framed to hang over the mantelpiece, sure that Joe would appreciate her. Joe would have preferred a picture of one of his own Shire mares, but was too well-mannered to say so.

He would shift the picture and have one of the January Queen and her foal. Maybe Nell would paint it. He liked the little picture she had done for Kate.

Nell, now coming over daily, was surprised to find how well her daughter organised her life. Cooking was done in the evenings, the radio on, food prepared for the next day. She and Joe both cleaned in the evenings too, keeping the amount of work to a minimum.

The days were for the animals. The sow and her piglets; the two goats that Joe had added to the ménage, both in kid; the cows and five bullocks that were now in the far field. Joe had made a kitchen garden; there were vegetables to pick and next year there would be fruit for jam and bottling.

'When we get going I'm buying a deep freeze,' Kate said, 'and we're having more sows; and adding another few cows. I'd like sheep in the farm field. I miss the sheep. And I want to breed dogs, then I can pick my own puppies and try and get what I want. Tearer might possibly make a stud dog, I don't know yet. I've been reading it up and listening to people talking and Joe knows a dickens of a lot about breeding. You should hear him talk about the Shires. I think I'll soon be able to judge a Shire mare myself!'

'A good brood bitch needs a head like a princess and a rump like a charwoman,' Nell said.

'Where did you learn that bit of lore?' Kate asked, amused and surprised.

'I overheard it at a dog show, the only one I ever went to with your father. He had an idea when you and Tim were small that we might breed English setters, but he decided against it in the end. We couldn't find one that was good enough for him. He's always been a perfectionist.'

He would hunt and hunt for a bitch as he'd hunted for a ram, Kate thought, and the memory of three thousand guineas wasted through her carelessness, brought depression to her mood. If she had that now . . .

The days passed swiftly.

It was years since Nell had had so much fun and Kate discovered that somewhere during the years, her mother had lost a sense of humour that was very similar to her own. Nell had recovered a light-heartedness she had long forgotten.

She scrubbed the filthy floors, enjoying seeing them come clean. She sanded the boards, and pulled off the paper, and Kate and Joe helped when there was time to spare. Ted came over in the evenings, and Bill, hearing of their project, decided to join in too. The evenings alone were bleak, and there was always laughter at Kate's.

Ted, telling Mick Brayshaw of the evenings spent at Kate's, persuaded his employer to come too. Mick proved to be clever with a paint brush and took over all the painting. He too had furniture he could spare. He was curious about this ménage: the old man, the Shire mare, and the girl. He was wary of Kate, who found him silent and awe-inspiring. He was fifteen years older than she. Almost her father's age. Mick would have been horrified if he had known how she regarded him.

They finished at nine each night, to give Joe time for a drink and some food and a rest before he drove back to the Home. Old Snorer was no longer so much of a menace. Joe's time in the attic room was limited. He would be able to move in next week.

The talk at night was always of horses.

The January Queen, and Mick's beauty, were to foal in

the same week. The hopes and dreams for them were very similar.

All the same, Mick was curious. He knew, and Ted knew, that the Shire mare could have been sold for far more than the knacker offered for her; that she should have been sent to one of the bigger auctions and not the tiny back street affair that she had been entered for; and he wondered why Joe hadn't tried to get her worth.

He asked Joe about it, as he was climbing into the land Rover.

'I didn't want money for her. I suppose I hoped that she wouldn't sell at all; I'd rather have shot her than had her in someone else's hands. Would you sell your mare? Even if you needed the money desperately? I hoped no one would bid for her—or she'd go to someone special—or the syndicate would think again.' Joe grinned. It had turned out far better than he'd hoped.

'I'd never sell my mare,' Mick said. 'She's the most valuable creature I own, and I don't mean financially.' The thought of losing her was unbearable. He brooded over her daily. Was she well? Was she in perfect health? Was she eating up? Was she walking well, or was there a trace of a limp? Was she exercised properly? He began to walk her himself, trusting no one. He fed her himself, so that he knew she ate every scrap and that she had all the extras a brood mare should have. He fondled her as she ate; he talked to her constantly, to get her used to his presence. He would be there all the time she foaled. She was already in the foaling block at night and he was sleeping in the room beside it, his ears ready for the least sound.

He wondered that Joe hadn't brought the Queen inside to the garage where there was room for a bed, but maybe the old man knew what he was doing. He certainly knew about horses.

When the mares foaled . . .

The days went by, and everyone regretted when the work was finished, except Joe. He gave a housewarming party, eager as a schoolboy to move in. The big room was painted white, chipboard paper covered in white paint on

143

the walls. Mick had brought two pictures, one of horses beneath trees, one of a galloping stallion—the picture of Ted's favourite mare had place of honour. Nell had painted the January Queen; she stood there, looking out from the canvas, her face serene. Nell had captured the expression in her eyes: a look of expectancy, and contentment, an odd look never seen in any but a beast about to give birth, a picture of serenity.

Nell had discovered curtains in a trunk up in the attic that fitted perfectly: old, peacock-coloured, tiny birds flaunting through forests of trees. Joe loved them. He had never had anything so beautiful before.

She had also brought two armchairs, and Ted had found a bookcase that he no longer needed. Mick had brought several chairs, and Nell had visited an auction for the bedroom furniture. There she brought home in triumph an old screen that she stripped of its paint, and covered in little drawings of her own. Farm animals ran all over it. Joe was delighted. It hid the bed and the wardrobe and chest of drawers she had bought for him.

The bathroom was painted, bright with colour; the little kitchen was red and white, mugs and cups hanging on hooks on the shelves, and Nell, who had always collected china and had far too much, brought over a box full. She added several pans, having more than she needed.

They all brought food for the party.

Nell made a big casserole. Ted and Mick contributed the drinks; Kate made flans and cheesecakes, scones and sponge cakes, eager to show her mother how well she could manage.

Nell was impressed and said so. She had told Charles about the party, but he wasn't sure if he'd be free. One of the younger cows was due to calf and it was her first. It depended on his ability to leave one of the men watching.

There was no need to break up early. Joe had moved in and was sleeping in his own home tonight. No more Old Snorer. His bedroom all to himself, no need to drive over in the morning. He'd be up when Monster yelled his greeting to the dawn, and out helping with the work. He and

Kate, they'd make their fortune; he'd a lifetime of experience to go on and she had her strength. She was a clever girl too. He would have liked her to be Ellie's daughter. Ellie would have loved to be here tonight, but if Ellie had lived then maybe none of this would have happened.

The thought astonished him, and he left them all, momentarily, as he considered the turns his life had taken; the events that influenced it and the way his path had changed. He'd lost interest in the farm when Mary died. No point in making more money than he needed, just enough to keep the mare and himself going.

Now, he needed money for Kate, and money to pay off those damned dilapidations. Matt had managed to persuade the syndicate to accept money weekly.

When he died. He'd no intention of doing that yet. Life was too interesting.

He returned to the present when a knocking came on the door.

Kate opened it.

'Dad!'

'Can anybody play?' he asked, putting down a box on the table. 'Bert said he'd stay till 10.30, so I can't be long.'

Kate lifted the lid to reveal an iced cake inside, the words 'Happy Landings, Joe' written in scarlet and a tiny model horse, a toy farm animal, standing on top.

'When did you get that made?' Nell asked, astonished.

'I went into the Plough for a drink and the landlady had made it. She thought someone would be in tonight to buy drinks for the party, and had it ready, but no one turned up. As I was on my way here, she gave it to me and said to call in tomorrow; the drinks will be on the house.'

Joe looked at the cake. He and Kate sometimes went into the Plough at lunchtime for a sandwich and a shandy for Kate and a bitter for him. They always talked to the landlady, who knew of their plans, but he had never thought her interested in them. She in her turn had developed a soft spot for the pair of them. It seemed hard on the child, on her own, but Kate was making out well; and the old man had always been one of Lily's favourites.

145

'Come and have a drink, Dad,' Kate said. 'It's a bit tag end-y, but Mick brought some sherry and Ted brought some home-made wine that's got a kick like a stallion's. Don't have much or you won't be fit to drive home.'

'Let's go and have a look at that cottage of yours, and see what we can by torchlight,' Charles said, a few minutes later after Kate had brought his drink. 'I've been dying of curiosity. Your mother's told me a bit. How are those sows? I'd have been over before but you know how it is.'

Kate did.

'Come and see.'

The animals blinked in the torchlight. Charles looked at the sties. Joe was a good workman and they were well designed and well made. Two of the sows had litters. Fine fat little pigs sucking busily, woken by the light.

Ten months since Kate had left home. She'd altered, matured, and had a confidence that amazed him. She'd grown up. He'd seen little of her in the months between; she'd been busy and so had he, and Nell always brought news of her.

Kate found herself talking eagerly, telling her father her plans: how she aimed to build up a small breeding unit of Shire mares—there was money in Shires. Charles knew that now; he had been making enquiries. Joe had taught Kate well. She knew her facts. She was changing her breed of pigs, buying in a new sow next week; and hoping to breed Jersey cows. Her first acquisition, a small Jersey calf with brilliant eyes, was lying on straw in the byre. That had been repaired and put into excellent order.

'I ought to have put you in as my tenant before,' Charles said.

Kate grinned at him, delighted to have him there.

There was no need for explanations; no need to remember. She knew now how much that ram had meant to her father. They stood in the stable, looking at the mare. Kate had brought her in an hour before. Joe had put in electric light so that they could watch her if need be when she foaled. The mare might be worth as much as the ram, if not more. She was the centre of their hopes for the future.

She was Kate's main investment. Charles, looking at his daughter as she stroked the soft neck, knew that Kate would make a farmer. Maybe she would take on his farm where he left off; even if she did add horses.

'Would you change over to horses and nothing else?' he asked.

Kate did not know the question was loaded.

'No,' she said, 'I enjoy the other animals too much; there's something very rewarding about having all sorts. Come and see my goats. They're our next venture. There's a demand for goat's milk from the health clinic and the hospitals for babies that can't digest cow's milk. And that means they can digest goat cheese and goat butter. It's fascinating. You start something and never know quite where it will lead. Look at Joe—I saw an old man selling a horse at an auction, and that's how that began.'

It began before then, Charles thought; it began with a madcap girl and a useless lout who killed a ram for me. And maybe it began before that, with Nell and me never giving them a chance to grow up.

It was hard to sort out beginnings.

'You're going to have the best foal that ever was, aren't you, my beauty,' Kate said, and the mare's head dipped to her shoulder, and the mare's cheek rubbed against her caressingly, accepting Kate now, as much her owner as Joe.

They went back to the bright room, blinking in the strong light. It was almost time to go. Mick was proposing a toast.

'To the January Queen and to my own mare and to both foals,' he said.

'To the best foals ever bred,' Joe said.

'To the foals . . . and their dams.'

Charles drained his glass, and turned to look at Kate. He caught the question in her eyes, and the worry. The thought had come unbidden to both of them, remembering the ram.

Anything could go wrong.

It wouldn't.

He grinned at Kate and she grinned back, and Joe felt

quiet satisfaction. It was good for a family to be to-gether—it was so much waste to have a daughter and never see her.

If Ellie had lived . . .

He pushed the thought away and concentrated on saying goodnight to everyone as there was a general movement towards the door.

Kate was last to go.

'OK, Joe?'

'Very OK,' he said.

'I'll help you clear up.'

'No. I want to do it alone. My own party in my own home. I haven't had a home of my own for almost a year. Let me enjoy the feeling.' He smiled at her.

She went down the steps and into the cottage.

It was comforting to look across the yard and see Joe's light, and to know that he was there to call on if there were any emergencies. Tearer came to her and nuzzled her hand, wanting affection. He'd been alone all evening. Too alone. The remains of her wicker wastepaper basket were strewn all over the floor. The paper in it had been torn to confetti. The wicker pieces were none of them more than two inches long, interspersed with the hard sticks on which the basket had been woven. Tearer, seeing Kate's expression, crept under a chair and refused to come out, his eyes watching her warily. It took Kate almost an hour to clear up. Tearer crept out, his whole body humble.

She stroked him and gave him his goodnight biscuits, and took him into the yard. She should have moved the basket and given him a bone to chew. He had been alone for a very long time.

Joe's lights were out.

She went to bed and lay thinking about the foal. When it was born she'd show it to her father, and she'd find out the price it would fetch at the top of the market. It it were a colt they'd have to sell it. She didn't want a male on the place. Not even gelded. If it were a filly foal they'd keep it and have two brood mares; then four; maybe more.

She'd sell to the States and maybe the oil countries

would be interested in Shires; she'd heard a rumour that they paid well. She and Joe would go places. And on his hundredth birthday they'd have a party to celebrate their good fortune.

She'd be over forty then. It was a very odd thought. An unimaginable age.

How did it feel to be so old? She thought of her mother, who in the past few days had seemed little older than herself. They had laughed together over the silly things that happened: Joe wrapped up in a piece of ceiling paper that fell and stuck to him; Kate, sitting backwards in a bucket that was luckily empty. Not even very funny incidents, but there had been a holiday air about all of them that came, she now realised, from Joe, who at the thought of his own home again had shed ten years and been imbued with new activity. It had been a good evening, but her brain was racing and it was a long time before she slept.

Joe could not sleep either.

He lay savouring the silence; it was too silent. He needed a cat, some creature to share the place with him at night when the bolts were drawn on the doors. He got up, uneasy, wondering if the mare were all right, and went out, taking his torch.

The Queen was resting, her eyes thoughtful.

He stroked her and she whickered softly, delighted to be visited in the middle of the night.

Joe left her at last and went back to bed. This time, he fell asleep quickly, comforted by the thought that he and the mare were close together again, that they were not separated by distance at night. If he was worried, he only had to go down the steps and across the yard. Kate was a good kid, but she didn't know much about the horses, and suppose the Queen foaled early? He drifted into dreams of foals—foals he had forgotten came to nuzzle him. He half woke. This foal would beat the lot of them; she would be the culmination of years of planning to get the right lines, the right temperament, the right conformation; a gentle mare, to breed good foals in her turn.

The Mare of the year.

The Mare of the century.

His name would go down in the history books of the breed.

Half asleep, he suddenly thought that life begins at eighty, and chuckled to himself. It was a long time since he'd felt so good.

## CHAPTER SIXTEEN

▶◆◆◆◆◆◆◆◀

Kate was learning fast. She had a future; she had a purpose; she had a raging need to show her father that she could farm as well as he. She spent the dark evenings immersed in the farming papers, reading the farming pages of their daily newspaper, or sitting in the Plough with Joe listening to the men talk.

She knew the prices of livestock and the variations every month; she knew the prices the beasts were raising in the cattle auctions and the sheep markets. She knew the price of feed. She knew how much they needed to supplement the cows. She had been alone to an auction and come back with a second Jersey calf. She and Joe had been penny-pinching for months to raise the money.

She sold eggs. She sold little pigs. She sold her bullocks. They fetched seven hundred pounds each and she and Joe had money in the bank at last. Three thousand five hundred pounds. They were rich. But the money had to go back into the farm.

More came from the little pigs, showing her a small profit overall. She would build more sties later and breed more pigs; but she wanted to increase her Jersey herd, and to breed Jerseys; and she wanted sheep.

What sheep?

She liked the Suffolks with their plushy wool and black heads; she liked the chunky bodies, and they had a good record.

'You don't want those, girl,' Bob Lennox from Horseshoe End said. Kate grinned at him. She liked Bob, with his endearing goblin face and wrinkled forehead and surprisingly brilliant blue eyes. He was a small man, like many of the other farmers; they seemed to be a small breed, she thought irrelevantly, looking round the room with contentment. Maybe her parents would come in later.

The Plough was over three hundred years old and had been cunningly renovated, losing none of its charm. It retained the old stone walls, the enormous fireplace with its arched roof and immense stone stack, and the worn flagged floors.

The settles were ancient pews from some long ago church. The bar counter was black oak, worn and scarred by centuries of use. Sam the landlord and Lily his wife collected china bulls and china German Shepherd dogs. Customers added their own offerings to the shelves that went round the top of the bar—six shelves, full of beasts. The model dogs, all of the same breed, were of all sizes and all shapes. Some were good specimens; some very much also-rans.

Under them, stuck by tacky pads, were pictures of customers' animals. One of Joe's prize-winning Shires; Bob's own Hereford bull that had taken all the honours at the last year's agricultural show; a winning ram from Leatherbarrow farm, which always upset Kate—she had to steel herself to look at it. Lily's own rosettes for her German Shepherd were there; she showed him in breed. He was a beautiful dog who sat behind the counter. No one knew he was there unless there was real trouble, when Colonel added his persuasion to Sam's. Lily and Sam ran a very quiet house; few wanted to risk an argument with Sam or his dog.

Kate was one of them now. One day photographs of her Shires would hang behind the counter too.

They had learned to respect her opinion, though she rarely gave it. She waited until she was sure of her facts, a

151

habit that enhanced her reputation with men who had been farming all their lives and were suspicious of a slip of a lass, even if her Dad was a pretty warm man.

'You want crossbreds,' Bob said, 'a good Mule, now.'

'The Texels are coming in and do well,' a small brown-faced farmer from outside the village said. He had come over to buy a young bull and stayed on for a pint before driving home. He had heard of Kate. Younger than his own daughter, and doing well out there on her own. He wondered how his Margaret would have made out if he'd put her down in a derelict cottage at the end of a lane and left her to it. He doubted if she'd have done anything at all. As it was she had stayed at home, worked on the pony stud down the road and was getting wed next April and that would be one mouth the less and one worry the less. He'd always been afraid she might give him a grandchild a bit soon like; and he didn't like modern ways at all.

'I don't want Texels,' Kate said. 'I like the Suffolks. Look what happened at the Abergavenny sale. The champion ram fetched over fourteen hundred guineas.'

'Rams like that don't come off trees,' one of the men said.

'Nor gooseberry bushes neither,' said the landlord, as he pulled a pint of beer and handed it frothing to the barmaid to carry to a far table. 'I reckon Kate knows where good rams come from.'

'I know,' Kate said, 'and next year I'll be driving down to pick myself one.' She didn't add that she was going to breed a ram better than the one her father had lost through her, and give it to him. It was another long-term project and one she was keeping dark, even from Joe. There were five big fields alongside her own, belonging to Mick. He wasn't using them, so maybe he'd rent them. She'd increase her acreage; she'd plans and to spare and she was beginning to have money to implement some of them. Though heaven knew it would take a dickens of a lot more to work it all out, as prices rose daily for animal feed, and nothing was certain.

She could get swine fever in her pigs; foot and mouth in her cattle; scrapie in her sheep; brucellosis; tuberculosis.

The ills that threatened were endless—foul in the foot and footrot; twin lamb disease and pulpy kidney. She'd been reading it all up and almost wished she hadn't.

'You're a bit young to know your onions, miss,' the farmer from beyond the village said, looking at Kate curiously. 'What did the reserve champion get at Abergavenny?'

'A thousand guineas,' Kate said. 'And the ewes averaged over a hundred pounds apiece; some of the better ewes were over two hundred pounds.'

He nodded.

'There's a demand for lambs just now,' he said. 'Now what have you got against the Texels?'

'They aren't so fertile as the Mules,' Kate said, 'or so some say. But it isn't that, I just fancy the Suffolks.' She didn't add that her father had a flock of Suffolks, and she wanted to breed him a ram—a wonderful ram to make up for the ram he had lost.

'You can't catch Kate out,' Joe said with a grin. 'I trained her myself. Eighty years of wisdom inside that dark head of hers; she learns fast.'

'What would you do about scrapie?' the farmer asked. 'I had a case myself last year; nasty.'

'You can't do much but cull them,' Kate said. 'They're no good for anything once they get that.'

'Would you know it if you saw it?' he asked her.

'The sheep would look a mess,' Kate said. 'Lose its fleece, go thin, no go in it, and loss of power in the legs. I doubt if you could miss it if you looked after your sheep properly.'

'You going to train your own sheepdogs?' Bob asked, grinning. He was pretty sure a woman would be no good at training a dog for the clocks.

'I might,' Kate said warily. She hadn't even considered a working dog, but she'd need one if she did go in for sheep in a big way, and the more she learned the more eager she was to increase her stock.

'She's her father's daughter; never beaten by anything,' the landlord said. He liked Kate. She came in almost every night now, just to sit, drink shandy and listen to the talk;

Joe made a pint last the whole evening and sometimes stayed on, but mostly he liked to make sure Kate got home safely. Hangman's Lane had a bad reputation and the village wasn't made up of angels.

The talk drifted to a dog that was worrying sheep on the other side of the village. No one had caught it yet.

Kate thought of that night, almost a year ago now, when her father had killed the collie that had been worrying his sheep. The beginning of a new life for her. No one would ever have thought that something so horrible could set anyone on a new path. It was a sobering thought; there were different choices to make daily. Suppose she chose Suffolks and brought back an infection with them; suppose she decided after all to try Texels; or settled for Mules. Each choice altered her life, took her in a new direction, as meeting Joe had taken her in an entirely different direction from any she had dreamed of.

Suppose she hadn't gone to the horse auction?

She would never have done as well; she would never have had the incentive to start up as she had started, would not have had Joe to teach her, to guide her and show her the way to do things she had never even thought about doing properly before. No one had ever had time to teach her the easy methods on her father's farm. They were always working against the clock. There were so many animals. Hundreds of sheep and over a hundred cows and forty pigs as well as the chickens and ducks and geese.

'Another bitter, Joe,' she suggested. 'Let's make the most of tonight; we'll soon be sitting watching the Queen to make sure she doesn't foal when we're out.'

'Just one,' Joe said.

He rarely had more than one but Kate had made a point. She had another shandy.

The talk turned to cattle; to bulls and to bullocks; to the changes made in farming by the Common Market. Joe had little time for the Common Market; he preferred the old days when the British farmer was on his own, not dictated to by things that happened elsewhere in the world.

'World's got too small,' someone said, holding up his

154

beer to the light. 'No head on this one, flat as that table there.'

'Fly from here to there in no time at all,' someone else said.

'It was better when they stuck to horses,' Ned Knacker said, surprising everyone, as no one had seen him come in. He tossed a coin down onto the counter and took his beer, and joined the group by the table.

'How's my beauty?' he asked Kate.

'Me or the mare?' Kate asked.

'The mare, lass, the mare. Would I want to know how you are, when I can see with my own eyes you're in fine fettle.' He grinned at her and winked.

'You've been somewhere else before now, Ned,' the landlord said. 'Take it easy.'

'I've been over at my niece's sampling her elderberry wine, is all,' Ned said. 'Don't know as it will mix with beer, but you're only young once.' He drank and choked with laughter.

'Put that pony down yet, Ned?' Bob asked.

'I did. Never seen such a rogue, or only once. I've the bruises on me to show it. Got a powerful backswipe from him.'

'I warned you,' Bob said.

'And I warned you when you bought him. Full of dope that pony was when I saw him. Gentle as they come, you said, but I knew better. Pity though to put down a young-ster like that. My old dad would have given him a chance; I haven't time. There's always some that goes bad though.'

He drained his glass.

'I'll try another.'

'That you won't,' the landlord said, 'and no one buys you one either. You've had as much as is good for you, Ned.'

'If you say so. You remind me of that pony. Nappy.' He considered his empty glass. 'Remember old Kipling?

Some are sulky, while some will plunge.
(*So ho! Steady! Stand still, you!*)
Some you must gentle, and some you must lunge.

155

(*There! There! Who wants to kill you?*)
Some—there are losses in every trade—
Will break their hearts ere bitted and made,
Will fight like fiends as the rope cuts hard,
And die dumb-mad in the breaking-yard.'


He turned his glass upside down and looked pleadingly at the landlord.

'No, Ned.' He wiped out three glasses, and filled them again for three impatient lads rapping their money on the counter. Someone fed a coin into the juke-box and voices were drowned in noise. The landlord flicked a switch and silence fell.

'We can have too much of that,' he said, silencing the complaints from the far corner. 'Need to hear ourselves think. I don't mind it when place is empty, but we're full tonight and folk come here to chat, not to have their ear-drums broken.'

Kate watched him. Sam was a big, heavy, slow-moving man until something happened to startle him into action, and then the cause of the action wondered just what had hit him, as he was swiftly grabbed by the collar and man-handled through the door and into the street. Sam had all the power of a bull and as much finesse as that animal. His ginger hair was spiky, his blue eyes wary, and he kept an eye on Kate's corner. Nobody offered so much as a flip remark to Kate in Sam's hearing. Kate was all right and he'd see she was never bothered.

'Time to go, Joe,' Kate said, glancing at the clock. It was necessary to be up very early to get through the work, and they needed sleep.

The men watched her go through the door, Joe behind her.

'Nice lass,' the farmer from outside the village said. 'Got some go in her, and she'll do well if the luck stays with her. You need a bit of luck.'

'If I'd had a bit of luck I'd have a field full of Shire mares by now,' Ned said wistfully, 'or a stud of me own. Like Mick Brayshaw. That mare of his . . . she makes my mouth water every time I see her.'

'Didn't know you ate horseflesh, Ned,' one of the lads said, grinning across at him, and lifting his glass teasingly.

'I do not. And you need a touch o' Kipling, son,' Ned said.

'I'm not your son, thank God. Kipling had whips, did he?'

'Kipling was a poet,' Ned said. 'Said a lot of sense and one thing he said was something my old man used to say to me:

> Ride with an idle whip, ride with an unused heel,
> But, once in a way, there will come a day
> When the colt must be taught to feel
> The lash that falls, and the curb that galls,
> And the sting of the rowelled steel.

Trouble with you youngsters is that no one uses the curb or the whip or the spur on you any more; you've all gone soft. If there were another war, what the 'eck would we fight with?'

'Time you went home, Ned,' Sam said and came and stood beside him. 'Go easy or do you want the lash that falls and the whip that galls and the sting of my fist down your ear'ole?'

'I'm going,' Ned said, getting up clumsily. 'And you got it wrong, mate. The flash that . . .'

Somebody laughed and Ned turned his head and glared.

'Come on, Ned.'

'Cool it, dad,' a voice said from the back of the room and Ned turned his head again, trying to see who had spoken. Sam took his arm and eased him out into the night.

'I hate putting a young beast down,' Ned said, revealing the cause of his unusual lapse into drinking. Sam remembered another night, four years ago, when he had had to drive Ned home. Ned had been called to a mare who had broken her leg beyond repair, a young mare in foal. A mare he had coveted for a long time. That night, Ned had quoted Kipling too; maybe the same verse—though not the second verse. Ned had to be watched when the young men were there; they riled him and he was too outspoken

157

for his own good. Luckily there wasn't much harm in the lads that came to his place.

He stood watching Ned walk down the road.

He turned to look into Hangman's Lane, where the trees grew thick and dark and the hedges seemed to overhang the road. He thought he saw a flicker of movement, but when he looked, it had gone. There always was something uncanny about the place. He wouldn't like a daughter of his living there.

They said bad luck loomed over it.

He had never mentioned it to anyone else. He wondered if Charles knew. He hoped that Kate didn't know.

Though she had all the luck in the world just now.

He went indoors.

'Daft old fool,' a contemptuous voice said from the back of the room and he wondered if it applied to him, or to Ned, or to neither of them. You learned to say nothing in his trade. He glanced at the clock.

'Time, gentlemen, please. Last orders.'

'That's a clever lass,' the farmer from outside the village observed.

Sam nodded. He wondered how much Kate owed to Joe. A hell of a lot, he reckoned.

## CHAPTER SEVENTEEN

▶◆◆◆◆◆◆◀

Joe never knew if he was witch-hunting, testing his luck, or if the uneasiness was born of long experience. He was grouchy the morning after the talk in the Plough, fidgeting round the Queen, looking for signs and tell-tales.

'Joe, what on earth is the matter?' Kate asked, beginning to feel edgy herself. Joe had visited the calf pens three times; had been out in the middle of his breakfast to look at the Queen, had gone to check the hen run to see if a fox had got in, had hunted out Monster, and examined his comb carefully.

'Something's up,' Joe said. 'Luck's held too long. There's something wrong, I know it in my bones.'

'Oh, Joe,' Kate said, exasperated. The old man must be going senile, and she didn't want that to happen. There wasn't a sign of illness or anything else wrong among the beasts.

She had added a new sow to her stock, and the sow was in an isolation pen right away from the rest of the beasts, just in case. Never knew what you bought in at times, Joe said. Could buy real trouble. Coul buy swine fever; could buy foot and mouth; could bring a mare to a stallion, infect him and make him useless. Could do the same with a dog. You never knew with livestock. They'd had it too good.

Kate began to witch-hunt too, looking at the goats, looking at the Queen. The new sow was a mistake. She had to admit that. But only to herself. She wasn't going to admit it to Joe. Outwardly the animal was everything a good brood sow should be, from her fat body, gleaming with health, to her attractive head and obvious good condition.

There had been very few bids for her. Kate got her cheap.

"Too cheap, my girl. I don't like it. She looks a damn good sow,' Joe said, 'but folk weren't bidding and they should have been—if I'd good stock I'd snap up this one. She's a beauty. As far as anyone can tell.'

Kate found Joe's gloomings more and more irritating. He stood often by the sty just looking at the sow. They named her Shara; and one morning Joe, coming after feeding her, flung down the swill bucket and swore.

'Should have named her Demon,' he said. 'She'd have had me on the floor if I hadn't been quick. You want to watch her. She's got a temper. That's why she went cheap. I hope that's all that's wrong.'

159

'She ought to farrow tomorrow,' Kate said. 'I've got the dates from her owner; he said she has a litter easily and is best left alone.'

'And I can see why,' Joe said. 'I don't like her, Kate. Don't like her at all.'

Kate found Shara far from endearing. She didn't mention her own experiences: a finger almost nipped to the bone, that she explained away by saying she had cut it with the chopping knife, and luckily it healed cleanly; and twice she had had to run out of the pen as the sow charged. She was a hefty sow.

Joe went back to look at the sow just before tea and came back with a white face and fury in his eyes.

'We get Ned and we get his gun,' he said. 'She's not staying another day, and we're not selling her. She's crazy.'

'Ned, she's about to farrow, we could hand rear the pigs. What's she done?'

'She's farrowed. And she's eaten every damned one; no wonder she was cheap. She's a cannibal mother; they come sometimes, and there's not much you can do. I'm not having her here. She's wicked and she's dangerous and she's useless. And she bit your finger, didn't she? You never cut it on any knife? Ned's coming over, as soon as he can make it. We'll be well rid of that one. She'll butcher well. Want the meat?'

'No, I do not want the meat. I'll have the money,' Kate said. She didn't want any part of the sow; didn't even want to think of her. The sty would be a fine old mess. She wouldn't fancy it ever again; and as for pigs . . . she looked at the other sows anxiously, but they came as always, snuffling and grunting, asking to be rubbed. Joe had fitted a tap in the corner of the pen, operated by pushing against it. The pigs could fill their own trough, by pressing the button. One of the small weaners had discovered the button and spent his time standing on his hindlegs, pushing his nose against it and washing his head, delighting in the running water. He was a pest, as he stood in the trough to work the tap and invariably mucked up the water with his dirty feet.

It was a relief to go out to the mare and stand beside her and stroke her. Suppose she ate her foal? Did mares ever kill their foals? Terrified by the thought, she ran to find Joe.

'Not the Queen. Things go wrong, but I never heard of a foal killed by the mare. I suppose it could happen,' Joe said, 'be more of an accident, I'd imagine.'

It wasn't a thought to brood on, but Joe was beginning to brood. They needed that foal. They needed the money for those piglets and the damned sow had eaten the lot; money down the drain. She was rampaging round the pen, enraged by any small action on the part of those who came near her. Ned took one look at her.

'Crazy as they come,' he said. He dealt with her and took the carcase away, as Joe hadn't wanted to touch her or take her down to Ned. Ned was coming back for a meal. He dropped in often, enjoying the informality of Kate's home where anyone was welcome. They were never made much of; if Kate and Joe were busy she yelled to them to put the kettle on and make tea and call them when it was ready.

Mick Brayshaw had begun to drop by too, to talk about his mare and stand with Joe, eyeing the Queen, looking at her coat, at her eyes, at her bearing, watching her walk, both of them ready for signs of trouble, both of them praying hard that trouble wouldn't arise.

The halcyon days ended and winter came with a bang and a bluster of high winds that tore tiles from the roofs. Rain poured daily from leaden skies and unharvested fields lay sodden. The river was rising. Kate eyed it anxiously. One day it was unnoticed, hidden, low between the rushy banks; then it was a ribbon of water, running fast, as it swelled, and then the pools began to form in the field. The Queen would have to stay in the yard.

Did the river ever rise that high?

She asked at the Plough and was reassured. It never reached further than the fence below her orchard. Never.

Joe now kept the Land Rover outside the garage, and at Mick and Ted's suggestion had turned the garage into a foaling box. It was divided by a wooden partition, on one side of which Joe now had a camp bed, a fan heater, a table and chair, and a power point that had once been part of a workshop bench, but that now served to heat a kettle. He kept coffee, biscuits and two packs of longlife milk on the table, and the bed was ready for use. The mare slept now in her stall, straw on the floor, the door made so that it could be opened wide. She came out for her exercise in the morning, slowly down the lane and back. And again before bed. She was massive now. Only a few weeks to go, only a few days to go. Mick's mare would foal four days later—he and Ted were never away from her now.

Winter was over before they knew it and February, flooding and rain-filled, ended, giving way to March. It had been a very short year.

'She'll foal tonight,' Joe said, looking at the mare. She was uneasy, often pausing and staring at nothing, or turning her head questioningly to look at her tail. She was restless, rustling the straw.

'I'll put her in the field for an hour or so at teatime; and then it's in for the night, fast,' Joe said. 'It won't happen yet. Might take her mind off it, to put her out for a little while. I don't want her to get too het up, though she's done it before and she foals easy.'

Nothing could go wrong with the mare.

Nothing.

Kate couldn't eat her lunch or her tea. She watched the mare, afraid there might be trouble. Was the foal the right way round? Was everything normal? Was the foal alive?

She went to talk to the Queen, to gentle her, soothe her. Tell her she was a wonderful mare. The wise eyes looked at her. The big head drooped confidingly to her shoulder.

'You'll be all right, girl,' Kate said.

It was almost time to put the mare in the stable. Kate washed up the tea things and Joe went to check the foaling box; he needed lubricant, disinfectant, a bucket of clean water, soap. He was busy finding them when he heard a roar in the sky.

He ran outside.

The supersonic boom deafened him. A window broke,

162

glass in the greenhouse broke, and the Queen ran. She ran ponderously, heavily, away from nightmare that came from the sky; monsters beyond imagining were up in the air; she had never seen anything that made such a noise; all she knew was that the world about her had exploded, that everything she had known up to then had betrayed her; devils and demons beyond imagining were there and she must get away from them.

Away from the house; away from the crashing glass; down the field and through the hedge; breaking it down as if it were made of sugar cane; into the flood meadow, until birth overtook her. Down by the river, oblivious to everything, the process speeded by her panic run, the Queen gave one almighty heave, and the foal came free.

It fell in the water.

The mare was standing in eight inches of water, just enough to cover the foal's nose. She stood, head down, sides heaving, too exhausted by her panic run and the disastrous birth to move.

Joe, tagging behind Kate who was speeding down the field, felt a pain in his chest and had to stop, wait for the pain to go and run on again. He came to find Kate frantically dragging the foal to clear ground, where she tried to give it artificial respiration.

He turned and went back to the house to phone.

He doubted if they could do anything now. He sat by the phone, his face grey. The vet, coming as fast as was possible, took one look at Joe and wondered if he had a patient here who needed more urgent treatment than the foal.

'Stay here, Joe.'

It was an order and Joe couldn't have disobeyed if he'd tried. He was too old to run, too old to farm. They were out to spoil life as they had always been—these men who made planes that could crash the sound barrier, and terrify the animals. He hadn't looked at the other beasts. They had only had one thought, for the mare. Down in the flooded field Vic worked with Kate.

'I'm sorry, Kate,' he said. It was bad luck. It was a filly foal and a little beauty.

163

He lifted it, and Kate led the mare slowly up the field.

The mare needed attention and the vet, glancing at Kate's stony face, decided it might be better to cure grief temporarily with major distraction.

'You've two invalids on your hands, Kate,' he said. 'It's up to you now whether the mare pulls through, and after that . . .'

Kate looked up at him and back at the mare. She looked sick and sorry and she had nosed the dead foal, now lying in the yard, and knew that she had nothing to cherish. Her head drooped even lower.

'Joe's knocked himself up, too,' Vic said. 'I'll see to the mare. Go and get Joe to bed. And ring for the doctor.'

He led the mare to the foaling quarters. Joe had made everything ready, and it was easy to start his work. He switched on the fan heater; the mare was wet to the hocks and shivering. He rubbed her down and bathed her; he fastened warm rugs over her, and she suffered him without seeming to notice that anything was being done for her.

Joe had insisted that Kate make the mare some oatmeal gruel with salt in it; never mind him, he hadn't just foaled. He was testy and he was desolate, but no use saying anything to Kate, who had set her heart on this foal. She did not want to think of it, lying there in the yard.

Another job for Ned Knacker. There'd be a bit of money. Who cared about that? It was a beautiful foal. Her throat ached when she looked at it on her way with the bucket of gruel.

'Good girl,' the vet said, in much the same tone as that he used on a sick dog. Kate looked as if she needed petting and patting. It was a damned shame. Bloody aeroplanes. It wasn't the first time a plane going through the sound barrier had created havoc, and it wouldn't be the last. The beasts might get used to it, in time; but the first time, even the second . . .

Neither he nor Kate realised that Joe was standing in the doorway. He looked down at the foal for a long time. She'd been a little beauty. All he'd hoped for, lying there dead.

He would have gone back to the flat, but it was too quiet, too lonely with his thoughts, and this time there was a niggling fear for himself. Kate needed him. His ticker couldn't pack up now, though it felt a bit as if it might, playing him up, racing and then slowing, so that he was aware of his heart and lay listening to it, as if it would suddenly stop without warning.

Better to be with people than on his own. Kate wouldn't leave the mare. So he would go to Kate.

'You can lie on that bed and be quiet, Joe,' Vic said, knowing why Joe was there, and worried by his appearance—he was breathless, holding on to the door as if he would fall without support.

It was better lying down; the light was bright and he could hear the mare moving.

'Is she OK?' he asked. He couldn't lose both of them.

'She will be. She needs a good deal of nursing. She's had one hell of a shock apart from the birth,' the vet said. 'Don't leave her alone.'

'I'll stay with her,' Joe said. 'Kate had better stay here tonight too, but I'll be fit in the morning. Shouldn't have run.'

The telephone was ringing.

Kate went out to answer it.

She listened to the voice at the other end.

'I'll tell him,' she said. She raced back to the foaling box.

'They want you at Brayshaw's—at the double, Ted says. He says it's disaster. Two horses with damaged legs and the mare's in trouble too.'

'That damned plane.'

He was into his van and away, tyres screaming, and Kate went back to the mare, to hold the bucket and coax her to finish the gruel. The vet had added brandy to it. Kate could smell the fumes.

'Could do with a snort of that myself,' Joe said, when the bucket was empty. Kate had rung the doctor. She made Joe and herself a cup of tea. Better not give him brandy till the doctor had been. She sat, listening to the alarm clock that stood on the table. Outside, day vanished and the stars came out.

She leaned back in the chair and slept, forgetting everything. Joe, listening to the sounds from the straw as the mare shifted, thought of all his life, leading up to this moment, to have his triumph snatched from him before it had even drawn breath.

The doctor, coming into the only light there was, looked at Kate, who hadn't woken; looked at the mare, who stared at him without acknowledging him, and looked at Joe. He had seen the foal.

'You're a fine lot,' he said. Kate woke and looked at him anxiously.

She slipped into the foaling box, and stood beside the Queen. Supposing she lost Joe and the Queen?

And what was happening at Brayshaw's?

That damned plane.

The vet arrived at Brayshaw's to find both Mick and Ted frantic. There had been mares in boxes, foals in the fields—and their most precious mare of all in her box, apparently safe, when the crash came from the sky. Two colts had raced, panic mad, down the field, tried to clear the fence and failed. Both had leg injuries.

Mick was in the stable with the mare. He hadn't repeated one swear word in five minutes and was still swearing monotonously and continuously when the vet came into the stable.

'Dear God,' he said.

The mare had reared in panic at the din and had hung herself. Her body was on the ground now. Mick had cut her down—her halter had caught on a hook that ought to have been beyond her reach. Heaven only knew how she'd done it, but horses could do the most extraordinary things. She hadn't had a hope.

'Can you save the foal?' Mick asked.

'I might.'

There wasn't time to talk. Everything was ready; the straw under the dead mare was clean. Lights had been brought to shine on her. Ted had organised fast, trying to salvage something from the disaster. No time to ask how long the mare had been dead; no time to do anything but start to cut into her, feeling her still warm body under his hands, swearing inwardly with Mick, hating civilisation that could bring such stupid calamities to innocent beasts.

The foal appeared under his hands.

It was still alive.

It twitched an ear as he cut the membrane round its face and cleared its nose.

It sneezed.

He lifted it and took it into the next-door stall away from the dead mare. Ted could tidy that up. No point wasting time on her. There was nothing he could do.

The foal needed to suckle. And fast. Vic looked up at Ted.

'Kate's mare lost her foal; the Queen bolted and gave birth by the river. The baby drowned. She's only foaled a couple of hours ago, she'll have the first milk for this little one. Want to try?'

'I'll try anything,' Mick said. He needed action, to forget that this mare he had brooded over with as much care as he would have brooded over a wife, was now dead. No more foals, no more morning conversations with her coming eager to greet him, whinnying over the fence, wanting his companionship more than that of anyone else.

No more winners from her.

No more prizes.

He looked up at the sky, innocent now. The danger was over, but it had left havoc in its trail.

They wrapped the foal in a huge rough towel and laid it on straw in the back of the Range Rover. The vet knelt beside it, steadying it, as Mick swung down the drive, into the lane and along it.

Hangman's lane.

Haunted lane.

Hateful lane.

Nothing good had happened to him while he lived here. And now Kate was touched with disaster too. It wasn't fair.

The vet lifted the foal out.

He and Mick stood beside the Queen's dead foal, looking down. Ned hadn't had time to come for it yet. They went to the foaling box.

Joe was asleep.

'How is he?' the vet asked.

'Just a bit tired, nothing to bother about, the doctor said. A couple of days's rest and he'll be as good as new.'

Kate's voice was exhausted—she had been up all night, trying to coax the Queen to feed. She stood, wrapped in rugs, warm, but interested in nothing. She did not respond when Kate stroked her or spoke to her. She would not eat and she would not drink.

Mick knelt and took up some of the soiled straw and rubbed it over his foal. It too was a filly foal.

The foal whickered, a plaintive hungry note.

The Queen turned her head. The vet lifted the foal and put it to her udder.

He was just in time to grab it back from the sideways thrust of a giant hoof. It was not her foal; it smelled wrong and she didn't want it.

Now they were in trouble, just when they thought there might be a solution for both animals.

## CHAPTER EIGHTEEN

◄►◄►◄►◄►◄

'Put the foal in the other stall for now,' Joe said. He had come into the stable, worried about Kate. In a long life, he had known bitter disappointment too often; Kate had never met it before. She stood, white faced, looking at the mare. Suppose she died too. Her hope for the future, all her money tied up in that one gamble; her need to breed good foals and her first foal dead.

Joe had a new bucket swinging by the handle. He went to the mare, and petted her, softly, soothingly, talking all the time.

'Whoa there, good girl there, steady now, steady. We can't leave you with all that milk; it'll never do and the baby needs it; if you won't give it to him we must; wait there, easy now little girl, little girl, easy, easy, easy,' and the milk was flowing under the old gnarled hands, as he bent to her.

She had always accepted him; had taken medicine from him, had allowed him to groom her, soothe her, feed her. He had bathed her after the birth, ignoring exhaustion, not quite trusting Kate to do it as well as he would. The milk flowed freely.

Kate watched it. There was enough for twin foals.

Mick was watching Kate, knowing how she felt.

'I had plans for my mare too,' he said, and Kate turned to him, at once sympathetic to his loss.

'Both of us—maybe we can salvage something. I can breed from my mare, and you have a foal.'

'I lost the best mare I ever had—it was only her second foal,' Mick said. It was a major disaster; insurance paid for horses, but money didn't replace the lost bloodstock. With both mares due to foal within hours of the event; both births a disaster, the Queen foaling early, in the wrong place, and his own mare rearing in terror, in a stable he thought completely safe. He would go through every stable that night, looking at hooks and hangings, make sure that in future the walls were completely clear. The mare had somehow managed to leap as well as rear— normally she could never have reached so high. Every time he shut his eyes he saw her hanging body, and swallowed bile.

Kate filled the feeding bottle that they used for calves. Mick was kneeling beside the foal which was sitting, its head weaving, ears pricked, reacting to every sound.

'At least it's a filly,' Joe said. Kate was busy, trying to insert the teat. The foal disliked the rubbery taste. She

169

squeezed so that warm milk flooded into his mouth; the baby swallowed, and then, after a few false starts, began to suck.

'That at least will keep her alive,' Vic said, relief in his voice. There were too many hazards; she was an orphan, delivered by Caesarean and likely suffering from shock. Joe had gone back to the Queen and put rugs over her. She could not stop shivering. She had been soaked by rain, had stood in water, had lost her foal, had lost her will to live—and Vic was afraid of pneumonia.

He looked at Mick and Joe and Kate; they seemed as much in need of treatment as the mare and foal. Joe had thought of pneumonia too; he was standing by the Queen, his hand on her neck, feeling her coat. He was sure she was running a temperature.

If he lost her, it would end for him too; his run had exhausted him, his heart seemed not to belong to him. It beat faster and then slow, and he was aware of it as he had never been before.

He hoped that no one else would notice. He was not leaving the Queen, whatever happened. He had to stay fit, she needed him; and it was him she turned towards, not Kate. Eight years together, it couldn't end now.

Mick and Kate were concentrating on the foal. It was impossible to neglect her needs, however much Kate was worried about the Queen. The foal needed mothering. She leaned confidingly against Mick, who was blindly computing the cost of the day's disasters—it was a fortune in money, and he didn't know where he would get a mare to replace the one he had lost. Maybe this filly in the future, but meantime he had lost his most prized possession. He had loved her, too; those that were left were nothing like the mare that had died. The others had been out in the fields, and though they had panicked they had room to run.

The foal too showed signs of shock. She had dropped to the straw after feeding and made little effort even to lift her head. She would need feeding day and night unless the Queen could be made to accept her. And Kate and Joe were exhausted; Vic had his own business to attend to;

and Mick had too much to do at home as well, though this foal was his major investment now, and he needed to make sure all went well.

He glanced at Kate.

She had turned her head away, wiping her eyes on her sleeve. She had hoped for so much; had planned for so much; and now it was ended. The Queen was a forlorn creature, reduced in less than half a day to an exhausted animal, caring about nothing, hanging head, and shivering body. The little foal now looked as if she too would take all their care to ensure that she lived.

'I'll be back later,' Vic said. He had to go, much as he wanted to stay. He had other patients: a sick cow beyond Ned Knacker's place, and one of Ned's own ponies with a leg torn by wire, also due to running, panic mad, when the plane went over. He had looked at the gash; it could wait, no vein or artery was cut, but it needed cleaning and the pony needed an injection, and he had to go back.

Sitting on the stool, watching the mare, Joe had slipped into the past. He was sitting as he once had sat beside the Queen's Treasure, after her foaling had lost her her foal. Ellie had been beside him, Ellie with her blue eyes and her ready laughter. She was standing beside him now, offering him a cup of scalding hot coffee, but her blue eyes were brown, eyes full of concern.

The past slipped away again. He took the cup from Kate.

'It'll all be the same in a hundred years, love,' he said. He couldn't think of any further consolation to offer. Nothing he could do for her or she for him or either of them for Mick.

Mick had slumped into the straw, knees almost under his chin, long and angular, his hair spiking untidily, his clothes stained with blood. Kate sat on the edge of the manger.

'You wonder why you bother,' Mick said bitterly. 'All that effort; all those years; all the planning; the breeding of the mare; the hunting for the perfect stallion; the perfect mating; the perfect foal. And in one afternoon it's all ended, stupidly, wantonly, unnecessarily. I don't know who was flying that plane, but by God, I'm making a stink about it.'

Joe hadn't the energy even to think of making a fuss. It had never occurred to Kate to do so. She thought of the night ahead; someone had to sit up with the Queen, and the foal needed feeding. She didn't know if she could take milk off the mare; she might well kick. It was Joe she adored. She was kind to Kate, but Kate wasn't her owner and never would be.

Suppose Joe died?

Would the mare accept her then?

Just now he looked as if he could well die soon; he was forcing himself to go on, his body protesting. He had never been so tired in his life, or felt so old. He felt a hundred, not eighty; he would have to rest but he couldn't leave Kate to manage alone.

There was the sound of a car in the yard. Brisk footsteps sounded outside on the cobbles. Charles bent his head as he came into the stable.

'The postman heard from Ned,' he said. 'Joe, you need to go to bed. Let me help out here.'

'With a horse, dad?' There was disbelief in Kate's voice.

'I know as much as any of the men, and I knew what you were going through,' Charles said. He glanced over the partition at the foal. 'Will it survive?'

'Anybody's guess is as good as yours,' Mick said. 'It fed, it's asleep, but the mare won't touch it and we're all resting till we have enough energy to try something else.'

'Ned's coming over to help,' Charles said, 'he's a wizard with those ponies of his. Get to bed, the lot of you, and let us take over. Kate, you're asleep on your feet; go to bed. Ned and I will do what needs to be done tonight. Is Vic coming back?'

Mick nodded.

'I'll be off, and thanks. I'll be over in the morning.' He had never known time drag so and yet it was late, after eleven. Bedtime was an hour ago. He was always up at six. He put his arm round Joe.

'Come on, off to bed. I'll come with you and tuck you in.' It was said in a rough voice, a stupid joke, but he

172

knew the old man needed help to get to bed and worry flared as he looked at him. Kate followed him out, but turned in the doorway.

'Dad, thanks,' she said.

He squeezed her shoulder.

'I know what it's like,' he said.

'The ram,' Kate said bitterly.

'That's in the past. I wasn't reminding you.' He had said the wrong thing; it was too easy to say the wrong thing.

'I was reminding myself,' Kate said. 'Maybe this is a sort of punishment. But it's showed me how you felt about the ram; that foal was my ram.'

'I know.' Charles could think of nothing comforting to say. Behind him the mare turned herself restlessly in the straw. He didn't like the look of her at all. He had been too long around stock to miss the signs of illness. And the foal was a small exhausted bundle stretched out in the straw, on the other side of the partition.

Ned came in, the tag end of a bottle of whisky in his hands and two glasses. 'Reckon we need it,' he said, as he poured. Charles was glad to drink; a small drink, easing the tiredness of the day from him. Ned screwed on the lid and put the bottle on the table. He glanced down at the foal.

'Looks as dead as the one in my trailer,' he said. 'Bloody shame.' He knelt in the straw and put his head against the foal's ribcage. 'It's breathing. Scare you stiff, sometimes, these little ones. How's Kate?'

'She's taking it hard,' Charles said, 'she always did.' He went to the mare, to look at her more closely. 'I'm not much use with horses.'

Ned went over to the mare and smoothed her neck.

'Hot as hell. What's she brewing up for us? Hope Vic isn't too late. I don't like it. Don't want Kate to lose the foal and the mare—she'd set her heart on breeding Shires and she'd got a winner.'

'Joe looks worse than the mare,' Charles said. He glanced into the yard. The light went out in Joe's flat and the front door shut. Kate walked slowly down the steps, Mick behind her. He paused, and put an arm round her, saying something to her. Kate leaned briefly against his shoulder, wanting company and contact, too tired to think or care about anything in the world.

Mick released her, and watched as she walked across the yard, almost stumbling with exhaustion. The front door shut behind her. He climbed into his car. He had to go home; he wanted to look at the rest of his stock, to see Ted and find out what further damage had been done. He was very aware of the empty stable as he drove in.

No head leaning over the open half door, no point in shutting it tonight. Not much point in anything. Everything he valued in life died on him: his wife died, his mares died, and now his foal would die. He lay in bed for a long time, too tired to sleep. He watched the moon slide behind dense cloud and appear again. The night sky was the colour of Kate's hair. Kate. Her face white, blue stains under her eyes, hair streaked with straw; Kate, kneeling beside the foal, intent on making him suck; Kate, passionate about horses.

Kate, warm against his shoulder, her cheek against his face; her image imposed itself between him and sleep. He must see more of Kate.

Kate.

He slept, totally exhausted, dreaming of nothing, and woke to a day he did not wish to live through, knowing that when he went down he would see the empty stable, and nothing would be left of his mare but her memory.

# CHAPTER NINETEEN

Kate, coming into the stable just after six in the morning, looked at Vic and Ned. They said nothing and she did not need to be told that the Queen was now a very sick mare. There was no life in her and she hung her head; her coat had lost its gloss and in spite of the rug on her back and the fan heater in the stable, she was shivering. The foal was standing, but its movements were lethargic. It took half the next feed and then refused to suck.

Vic had spent two hours in the stable with Ned, trying to make the mare accept the foal. Ned had haltered her, and Charles held her while she was milked—the foal had to be fed somehow. They tried to hold her still and force her to feed the baby, but she would have none of them and they dared not wake Joe.

The foal, to crown it all, was constipated; and this alone was a major problem at her age. Vic put a tiny dose of castor oil into the milk. He did not want to take more drastic measures.

Ned tried smearing the foal with straw from under the mare. She ignored her. The mare turned her head away, and once again her hoof threatened and the foal was hastily removed. Charles made up her feeds, but she refused those too.

Kate went to cook breakfast for all of them. She was worried about Joe, but he came down soon after seven, and sat in the chair by the fire, holding his hands to the blaze.

'Doesn't look good,' he said.

Kate said nothing. She dished bacon and eggs as Charles and Ned came in, and poured coffee. Mick, arriving a few minutes later, looked longingly at the food.

'Had breakfast?' Kate asked.

He shook his head. He had been in to look at the mare and the foal, and was even more worried. He was also hungry. Kate added three rashers and two eggs to the pan, her mind on the mare. Vic took over the pan from Kate and made her sit down and eat.

'Let me,' he said, flicking over an egg expertly. 'We have to find some way of making that mare take to the foal; it will cure her quicker than anything to have a baby to think about. She's mourning, as much as sick.'

'Dare we mate her again when she comes in?' Joe asked. She'd normally go to the stallion when the foal was a few days old.

'Have to see.' Vic wasn't saying until he knew how she was faring. At the moment she wasn't fit to travel; she wasn't fit for anything.

He went out to the stable, and jumped as two pigeons flew from behind the mare, having been picking through the straw for food. There was a nest behind the manger that he hadn't noticed. Pigeons would nest anywhere, and feed anywhere.

The foal was asleep again.

Joe was trying to get the mare to feed, coaxing her and soothing her. He couldn't rest, though he knew he should. No one else could manage her as he could. She nibbled gently, and then turned away her head.

'At least she drank a little,' Joe said. He had had the bucket standing near the heat to get the chill off the newly drawn water. Water would keep her alive.

When Joe returned to the kitchen, Nell was there, washing up the dishes and ordering Kate about as if she were a little girl again, trying to break through her misery.

Mick had looked in at the foal, had a word with Victor and gone back to his own affairs. There was never time to spare. Horses to be fed and exercised, day in and day out. Other mares to care for; other foals to watch over and his field of yearlings to be supervised. Horses were daft beasts, startled by a mere nothing, let alone a supersonic boom, and apt to run into obstacles instead of jumping over them and clearing them. One, only last year, had run into a tree and almost blinded himself on a twig that speared his eye; another had jumped wire and torn his belly. Legs seemed to get gashed whenever the wind blew, and lads chucking glass around injured more horses than anyone could count.

He went into his office and turned up his veterinary dictionary. Diseases of foals: constipation, which could kill; diarrhoea which could kill; salmonella causing paratyphoid, which could kill; rupture which could kill. The mare's milk could cause problems if she were ill or wrongly fed, so maybe they shouldn't persist with trying to foster this one on the Queen. Worms, blood poisoning, pneumonia. He stared at the pages, wishing he hadn't bothered.

'For God's sake,' said Ted, coming into the office with a sheaf of bills. 'You'll drive yourself crazy. The foal will survive, and so will the Queen. Only needs time and nursing.'

'You haven't seen them,' Mick said.

'I'm going down now. Where's the paraffin oil?'

'There's some in the cupboard in the tack room.' Mick kept a hunter for riding; and Ted had his own mare for hacking around the lanes whenever he had time. Both of them hunted on occasion, enjoying the exercise and the excitement; following the hounds gave a good day's riding.

Mick closed the book, and went back to work. Ted drove down to Hangman's Lane. He went into the stable. The mare turned her head towards him.

'Tried everything,' Joe said.

'You haven't tried this,' Ted said, rubbing paraffin oil onto his hand. He smeared it over the mare's chest and then, talking softly to her, rubbed more of it over her nostrils and her soft muzzle. She licked at the oil tentatively. He had a honey jar in his car, and brought out the honey; he rubbed that too over her, and put some on his hand. She licked at it.

He went to the foal.

He rubbed it along its back, along its neck, along its tail; he rubbed it underneath and he rubbed its promise of a mane; he rubbed honey round its lips and its tongue savoured the sweetness. He bent to the mare; her hoof came back and he handed the honey jar to Joe.

'Get it on your hands and then stroke the udder,' he said.

Joe, remembering back, wondered why he hadn't tried honey. The mare loved it and he sometimes put it in her feed. Honey was good for many things. Well loved by country people. He took honey and cider vinegar to keep off his rheumatism.

He held the mare, and Ted lifted the foal and held its head to her udder. It began to suck, and as the milk came, it sucked more strongly. The mare moved restlessly and Ted shifted his position and held the foal's head to the mare's head.

She sniffed; the foal smelled as her lips and muzzle smelled, and smelled of her own milk. She licked, and licked again. Ted put the foal down in the straw.

The Queen watched it, as it staggered muzzily, came to stare up at her, and then to stare at the strange room in which it found itself. The stall in which it had first been put was dark, but light filtered in to the mare's stable. The foal sniffed the manger and the water bucket and then collapsed on rubbery legs. The mare nosed it again.

'Best to go easy,' Ted said, lifting the foal and settling it down again on clean straw in its own stall. 'Try her with food now.'

The mare licked at the gruel. Her interest had been roused; the dormant mother instinct had been awakened. She was not yet sure about the foal, but she no longer tried to kick it. Ted sponged her udder, and then rubbed the sponge on the foal's head.

'Softly, softly,' he said, as he shut the stable door behind him, and offered his arm to Joe. Joe, watching the mare's interest roused, seeing a change in her when the foal sucked, was beginning to feel better. He would rest today, but that was all. He went into the kitchen and sat by the fire, while Kate busied herself with the other stock and Nell began a huge baking, to tide them over while they were both busy with the mare.

Nobody noticed Tearer make his way into the Queen's stable.

Tearer was part of her familiar life; she nosed the dog, and he licked her muzzle, liking the taste of honey. He brought her reassurance and comfort and, when Joe and Ted went out to the foal again, Tearer was curled up in the straw against the mare, who had her head alongside his head and was resting quietly, all signs of shivering stopped.

The dog watched with interest as the foal was brought in; he watched as the Queen licked the small head; and this time, when the foal went to suck, she made no move to kick. When the baby had finished, the mare licked her mouth clean, and licked her whole body. Again Ted sponged the mare's udder and rubbed the sponge over the baby.

They weren't out of trouble yet.

It might not be safe to leave the baby with the mare, she might still reject it or harm it; they had to watch, all the time. Also the Queen still had a slight temperature. Kate brought her a fresh baked granary roll, just a taste. She loved new bread and it tempted her, stimulating her salivary juices so that when Joe offered her yet more gruel, she drank it all.

Patience.

Vic said the word, as he watched Kate hold the foal, watched Ted, or Mick, or Charles hold the mare, watched those giant legs, that with one swift kick might well end the life of this baby. She was beautiful.

No one could see enough of her; of her delicate body, her fine legs, her miniscule mane and tail, her small head. She was daintiness brought to reality—even daintier beside the mare, who seemed a giantess in comparison.

One kick . . .

Kate could not sleep. If she closed her eyes she saw visions—visions of Mick's foal lying dead as the Queen's foal had been, but this foal was mutilated, kicked to death by the Queen. She brooded endlessly over the stable door, unable to finish her chores, looking to Joe for reassurance, wishing Mick would come over and stay there, beside his own foal.

He had told her its value and that didn't help at all.

There would be insurance to claim on the mare. Insurance didn't replace blood lines, didn't replace flesh and blood, didn't make up for an empty stable—that made Mick feel more bitter every time he passed the door. Ted was surly too, feeling the hook on which the mare had been hung had been his fault. He should have thought, should have looked, should have inspected every inch of that box, but he hadn't. The hook was high. If the mare hadn't leaped . . . if the plane hadn't gone over . . . if the sea were green cheese and the moon made of pepper . . .

He was going daft.

He didn't realise he was almost dead on his feet. They were short staffed without Mick, who was brooding over the foal, as terrified as Kate that the mare might injure it. But they needed her milk.

They never left the baby alone with her. Joe, now creeping around, beginning to feel less likely to die before his time, which he had decided was around a hundred, was back with them whenever he could persuade them to let him into the stable, talking to her, coaxing her, giving her extra feed; trying to build her confidence. She was letting the baby feed, but somehow she had not yet attached to it.

She suffered it. That was all.

Tearer, jealous of the attention given to the horses, spent much of his time in the straw. He enjoyed lying beside the foal; his yellow coat against her chestnut coat. He licked the milk from her lips and she was comforted by the dog and less lonely.

Kate was like a sleepwalker. She had never been so tired in her life.

There was too much to do, all the time. Extra feeds to prepare for the mare. The big sow had farrowed and had no milk. Told you not to buy her, Joe said, not helping at all. He'd been sure she was a no good buy and they'd already had one bad bargain. Kate had to learn; he let her go to the sales alone. There'd been something about this one. He didn't know what. It took years to know a good beast. He couldn't teach that to Kate.

A non-doer, and ten little pigs to bottle feed.

As if they hadn't enough to do.

Sell them as sucking pigs, Ted suggested. Kate was appalled.

It was bad enough to sell them as weaners; she hated selling her stock.

Patience.

Ned said it as he came to help, standing beside her while she watched over the foal, a little nervous herself, lest the Queen decided to kick. The Queen was improving in health but she wasn't right yet. She had a cough that worried Vic, and that meant more treatment, which took time.

Time.

Time to feed the hens; to let them out and let them in and collect the eggs.

Time to chase the cock, who had decided to go adventuring and see if there were more hens further afield.

Time to muck out the pigsties and feed the little pigs; to make up swill for the sows; to watch over their second sow, soon to farrow; to make extra feeds for the Queen; to make her tonics; to make food for herself and Joe. Nell came over daily, bringing cakes and soups and pies, but food still had to be heated; vegetables had to be prepared, and Nell had her own home to see to and the men to feed.

She sent thermos flasks of soup with Charles. Mick's housekeeper made bread for them, and added cakes and scones; and came over twice a week to cook a big meal and see they had something inside them. Mick rarely spoke; he was bitter and angry and resentful. He stared at the sky, as if afraid another plane might come and cause another disaster.

Every stable had been checked; the big paddock had been cleared of obstacles; the fences were being raised, so that the colts couldn't jump them; the fields were checked daily for wire and glass, flung over by passing idiots. People were for ever throwing things over hedges, or opening his gates and driving cars on to his fields to picnic, as if every field in the country were public property.

A foal ate polythene and almost died.

A colt cut its leg on a beer bottle, which it broke as it cantered free, along the hedge.

Mick began to hate people even more than before.

He spent more time with the foal. He brooded over it, watching it. Would it catch the Queen's cough? The vet had said not. Would the Queen harm it? None of them knew. Would it survive? Was it growing? It didn't seem to be any larger. It was so tiny standing there beside the Queen, drawing milk from her huge udder.

Kate had fallen in love with it.

Even Joe was now as proud of the foal as if it had belonged to his own mare. Ted came daily, to watch over its progress, and Charles, intrigued in spite of himself, came over as often as he could find time.

'That foal might have been worth three thousand pounds,' Kate said forlornly, reading the Farmer's Guardian.

Charles nodded. He had shopped for Kate and Joe, knowing Kate would not have time. He took two of the feeding bottles for the little pigs.

'Did yourself no good at all with that sow,' he said. looking at her. She was fat and greedy, ignoring her young. She would have to go—a sow who couldn't provide milk was no good to anyone.

'There's so much to learn,' Kate said forlornly, 'but at least these are thriving.' The little pigs were around her, squealing for their bottles. They suckled the food down as if they had never been fed before. 'And at least they were easier to feed than the Morsel.'

Charles grinned.

'Who named her?'

'Joe. He looked her over when he first saw her and said "She's nobbut a morsel after a Shire foal", and the name stuck. Vic's sure she'll make it now. But we can't take the Queen to the stallion. She isn't fit. And it's such a long time to our own foal.'

She took the bottles indoors and put them to soak in the steriliser. Charles had brought over one of his to make the job easier. Before that Kate had to use boiling water, and the job took ages.

She stood in the yard looking around her. Nobody would imagine it was the same cottage. Neat and tidy, the wood painted, the garden dug, ready for planting; the sheds and stable and sties all shipshape from Joe's work, and with Ted's help, it was a long way from the slum it had been when she first took over.

'You've done well,' Charles said, joining her, and guessing her thoughts.

Kate walked over to the stable. It was a day filled with bright sunshine, a warm day, and Ted was leading the Morsel out into the yard. She had never been outside before, and she looked about her, her wide eyes curious. She saw the trees, and shied.

Ted laughed.

'She'll do,' he said. 'Look how solid she is on her legs now. She's beginning to grow; I hadn't noticed before.'

Tearer was chasing his tail, suddenly filled with excitement. He raced round the yard, his hard little body speeding full out, tail streaming behind him. His ears were flat against his head. The foal bucked and whinnied to him. She wanted to run.

From behind them, in the stable, came an eager reply.

The Queen was calling to the Morsel.

The foal answered.

The Queen thrust her head over the stable door, her eyes anxious. They had taken this baby out into the yard on its own, and the latent mother instinct was roused as it had not been roused before. She wanted to supervise.

She whinnied again, and the foal replied.

Joe, his eyes suddenly bright, opened the half door and led the Queen into the yard.

She went at once to the foal, moving slowly and ponderously, and nosed the baby's head. The foal lifted her nose to the Queen, and then turned to suck. The big head watched her. The foal finished her feed, and turned back to her foster mother.

The Queen began to lick. Lick over the head and the body; lick the foal clean, lick as if she had never been able to lick properly before, from nose to tail and back again.

Joe grinned, his mouth stretching. The Queen was on the mend and they'd have a foal off her in a year's time, or a bit more; a good foal.

Mick grabbed Kate and kissed her.

Ted beat a fist into his hand and Charles, watching, found himself grinning too.

Vic, driving into the yard, wondered if he was confronted by lunatics. Mick and Kate were laughing, Charles was grinning at Joe and Ted was doing a hornpipe with Tearer, holding the dog by his front paws. The dog, crazy with pleasure at being noticed after all this time, was barking and the cock, incensed by the frenzy around him, had flown to the top of the henhouse and was crowing discordantly.

'The Queen's accepted the Morsel,' Ted said, dropping Tearer's paws. 'Look at them.'

Vic looked.

The Queen was moving towards the gate of the big paddock, her old haunt. It was time to show her baby the world. She waited as Kate unfastened the gate, and led the Morsel in. They stood, the enormous mare and the tiny racehorse foal, looking back at the people they had come to know so well. The foal danced towards the gate and thrust her muzzle into Kate's hand.

Then, overcome with joy, she began to buck, until everyone in the yard was laughing at her, euphoric with relief.

'We'll celebrate,' Mick said, 'down at the Plough. We can leave them safely together now; and we'll have a meal to remember. I'll go off and book it now. They put on a good spread. Bring Nell,' he said, over his shoulder, to Charles, who by now was a crony, having suffered sleepless nights and anxiety with them.

'You OK, Joe?' Kate asked, when the men had gone off to pick up their own affairs.

'Never better,' Joe said. 'Next year . . . we'll do better . . . there's the chance of a young stallion that's been

184

making the headlines; reckon he might give us an even better colt.'

There was always the future; to plan for, to hope for; and Joe, sitting down to go over their accounts, came up with a profit—money in the bank. He showed the books to Kate, as she came down ready for Mick's party.

'We've something to celebrate,' he said, 'even with losing the foal. The pigs and the cattle have shown a profit, and there's a chance of that new young ram from Ned's brother. A Jacob ram; put him at stud . . .'

Kate nodded.

She was learning to be cautious; not to plan too closely; to think of the possible problems, as well as the possible rewards. She glanced into the stable before they went out. The mare was standing beside the tiny foal; two shadows blended. Tearer lay in the straw beyond them, watching over them.

She left him free.

He was a good guard dog.

Joe eyed her as she climbed into the Land Rover. She had dressed carefully; a long dress, and a ribbon in her hair. She was a right pretty lass when she was dressed as a lass. He let in the clutch and drove skilfully out into the lane. He wasn't finished yet.

Not by a long chalk.

## CHAPTER TWENTY

▶◆◆◆◆◆◆◀

The Plough was crowded. The smoky air met them, almost choking Kate. She saw her parents by the bar, with Ted and Mick, and fought her way through the men, many of them turning an appreciative eye, of which she was quite unaware.

'Everything OK?' Mick said.

'They're fine,' Kate said, knowing what he meant. For them, there were only two animals in the world; the Queen and the Morsel. Their future. In time, they would forget their losses. Tonight, they were celebrating a new beginning for both animals.

Ned joined them, and Vic came with Marie, his wife, who helped him with the practice, giving anaesthetics, holding animals, endlessly on the phone, making up his books for him, taking notes when he was out on a long job, or doing the TT testing.

The little room was laid out with flowers on the table. Melon soaked in port, topped with cherries; a soup that made Nell ask for the recipe; roast duckling with orange sauce and a delicious stuffing that defied any attempt at analysis; tiny roast rounds of potato and peas from the freezer; a meringue mountain topped with fruit and cream; coffee and mint crisps, with cream in bitter chocolate cups that were delectable to eat when emptied. Charles bought the wine and Ned bought brandy for everyone.

They had the room to themselves. It was a small room, the ceiling low raftered; the walls panelled in dark wood, hung with pistols and swords, with cutlasses and sabres, with horse brasses, and hunting horns. Hunting prints were on the walls; a bright fire blazed in an iron basket.

'To the Queen and the Morsel,' Vic said, lifting his glass.

They drank solemnly.

'Kate and I have made a pact,' Mick said. 'Without the Queen, my foal might well be dead. I've the room and know-how. She's agreed to a partnership. I'm buying another Shire mare with the money I owe for fostering, and Kate's renting the big paddock that runs alongside her fields. I've been offered a good mare in foal—Ted's been asking.'

'Sounds like a good idea,' Charles said.

'The mare's on her way. There's a future in Shires, but Kate can't manage on her own; she's enough to do. I've the men and the space, and we're close neighbours. Kate's going to learn from Ted, and from me. Joe can have one of my men to help out with the chores. I've two students who want to be farmers later, and we get students wanting to be vets; they can learn from Kate's place— smallholdings don't usually give much chance to that type of man. It'd be good for them to learn what goes on, especially those that are going into practice. We think it's a good idea.'

'It is,' Vic agreed. It had been a good evening. A colleague was standing in for him and he had the night off. No night calls. It was a night to remember: harbour after storm, peace after the long worry, and the fear that they'd lose both mare and foal.

'Kate and I need to talk things over,' Mick said, and handed Kate her shawl. She followed him meekly, and Nell looked at Charles. They had no need to speak. Joe, seeing the glance, knew what was in their minds. It was early days; and Mick was older than Kate, but . . .

He said nothing, and toasted his thought in secret, staring into the fire. He was very tired. An old man, his future secure.

Outside, Kate stood looking into a sky free from cloud.

'Where shall we go?' Mick asked.

'To look at the Queen and the Morsel, where else?' Kate said.

The moon shone brightly over Hangman's Lane. Mick wondered how he could ever have thought it haunted. Trees cast long shadows. An owl hooted as they drew up by the gate of Willow Cottage and Tearer came to greet them, every inch of his body wagging, his teeth bared in an agonised smile, trying hard to tell them how glad he was to see them home.

The Queen was lying in the straw, the foal tucked against her. She lifted a sleepy head. The foal's ears flickered, but she was sound asleep, full fed, and tired out by her first day outside.

Kate bent to stroke the Queen's soft neck.

Mick looked down at her, but did not move.

Kate.

He looked up into the night sky; and the moon and the bright stars were there, as they had been for centuries.

There was all the time in the world. There was a future, but he'd take it slowly.

He no longer believed in rushing his fences.

Patience.

Kate, unaware of his thoughts, straightened herself and smiled at him. He was her partner in horses; she would learn from him all that he had to teach. One day her name would be as famous as that of her grandfather. Simon Malone's granddaughter. Kate Malone. Mick looked at her, planning that they would both be known. Mick and Kate Brayshaw. He looked down at the foal, as Kate fastened the door. His future; Kate's future; the foal's future; and the Queen's future.

The January Queen.

If it hadn't been for her, they would never have met. If the plane hadn't flown over, and they had not lost their animals . . . it was odd how things turned out.

Joe, driving into the yard, saw them standing together. He smiled to himself and called a goodnight. There was a parcel on his doorstep. He bent to pick it up and took it indoors, wondering about it.

Nell had called on her way to the Plough.

He unwrapped the parcel and set the picture on the table against the wall.

The great mare brooded over the tiny foal.

The January Queen and the Morsel.

He hung it on the wall, unaware that by next year the picture would have pride of place at the Royal Academy, the day that Mick and Kate were married. He looked at it for a long time before he turned out the light.

He smiled to himself in the darkness, and that was how Kate found him in the morning, lying quietly.

He would never wake again.

She went downstairs to phone Mick. He came over, and they stood for a long time together beside the old man, forgetting for the moment that there were things to do and animals to be fed.

Joe had given her the January Queen; had brought her a future.

'He had the best months of his life because of you,' Ned told her, as they left the church after the funeral. They had led the Queen behind the procession. Kate wondered if the big black mare was aware that she had lost her master.

That night the Queen came to Kate and stood against her, leaning her head on Kate's shoulder. It was strange without Joe, but she was no longer lonely. Mick was down the road and would come if she phoned for him. In a few more months they'd be together. She took that for granted now. Mick was half of her life. They belonged together.

She closed the stable door.

Her mother's picture stood on her dresser, a last memory of Joe. The Queen was hers, and would never know another owner. That night when she went up to bed she took Tearer with her. His soft breathing was comfort in the empty room. She was too aware of the deserted flat across the yard, and the dark windows; and the silence in the morning, knowing that Joe would never again come down the steps and greet her with his smile, and quiet companionship.

She slept and dreamed of a racehorse running; and a big Shire mare standing patient in the paddock while the foal that she had fostered sped away from her to a life that the Queen could never even imagine.

**CASEY**
by Joyce Stranger

The touching story of a cat with a difference.

Life at Wayman's Corner could never be dull. Crises lurked around every corner . . . marital friction, careless city visitors, farmyard accidents, and Casey.

Casey, son of a Siamese tomcat and a black farmcat, was an animal with great determination, strong affections, and a nose for mischief, whose strange friendship with Sultan, the terrifying Jersey bull, becomes a central part of life on the farm . . .

0 552 10125 7     85p

**KYM**
by Joyce Stranger

Joyce Stranger's novels have become well-loved favourites with all age groups. Her first non-fiction book is sure to take its place among them.

*Kym* is the autobiography of her Siamese cat who, for thirteen years, adored her, dominated her, and played havoc with her life. A more accident-prone cat never lived. Even on holiday he managed to turn their caravan into an ambulance—or a peepshow. A born eccentric and voluble talker, a cat with the grace of a dancer and the instincts of a prizefighter.

An endearing story of the misadventures of a unique pet, seen through Kym's blue-eyed squint, and his owner's humorous and observant eyes.

0 552 10695 X     85p

## RUSTY
### by Joyce Stranger

A powerful and impressive story. Joyce Stranger is absolutely honest with her characters, and they are all the more attractive for such treatment. . . . Rusty himself is no semi-human pet, but a real stag with dangerous habits and barely suppressed instincts. . . .

The story is full of excitement, and though, like any honest animal story from *Black Beauty* onwards, it is bound to be tragic, there is also plenty of humour, and the ending is full of hope.

0 552 10126 5      75p


## NEVER TELL A SECRET
### by Joyce Stranger

Life at Shallow Dene Farm had never been easy, but 12-year old Shanie was used to helping her father and caring for the animals. Somehow, they managed to get by. Then suddenly, in one terrible afternoon, the peace of the little farm was shattered: vandals from the nearby town arrived on motorbikes and as well as stealing from the house, they killed and injured many of the animals.

Shanie was heartbroken, but as the weeks went on, she discovered that one of the cats who had lost her kittens in the raid had made a home in an old haunted house, and had adopted two orphans—a kitten. . . . and a fox cub. Shanie decided that the little family needed protecting—and she was determined to keep this secret to herself. . . .

0 552 10397 7      85p

# A SELECTED LIST OF FINE NOVELS
# THAT APPEAR IN CORGI

| ☐ 11160 0 | THE CINDER PATH | *Catherine Cookson* £1.25 |
|---|---|---|
| ☐ 10916 9 | THE GIRL | *Catherine Cookson* £1.50 |
| ☐ 11202 X | THE TIDE OF LIFE | *Catherine Cookson* £1.50 |
| ☐ 11374 3 | THE GAMBLING MAN | *Catherine Cookson* £1.25 |
| ☐ 11368 9 | THE FIFTEEN STREETS | *Catherine Cookson* £1.00 |
| ☐ 11449 9 | MAGGIE ROWAN | *Catherine Cookson* £1.25 |
| ☐ 11260 7 | THE INVITATION | *Catherine Cookson* £1.25 |
| ☐ 09074 3 | LOVE AND MARY ANN | *Catherine Cookson* 95p |
| ☐ 09075 1 | LIFE AND MARY ANN | *Catherine Cookson* 95p |
| ☐ 09076 X | MARRIAGE AND MARY ANN | *Catherine Cookson* 95p |
| ☐ 11335 2 | KATIE MULHOLLAND | *Catherine Cookson* £1.50 |
| ☐ 08849 8 | THE GLASS VIRGIN | *Catherine Cookson* £1.25 |
| ☐ 11203 8 | THE DWELLING PLACE | *Catherine Cookson* £1.25 |
| ☐ 09318 1 | FEATHERS IN THE FIRE | *Catherine Cookson* £1.25 |
| ☐ 09373 4 | OUR KATE | *Catherine Cookson* £1.00 |
| ☐ 11205 4 | THE SLOW AWAKENING | *Catherine Marchant* £1.25 |
| ☐ 11372 7 | HOUSE OF MEN | *Catherine Marchant* £1.25 |
| ☐ 11371 9 | THE FEN TIGER | *Catherine Marchant* £1.00 |
| ☐ 10375 6 | CSARDAS | *Diane Pearson* £1.95 |
| ☐ 10249 0 | BRIDE OF TANCRED | *Diane Pearson* 85p |
| ☐ 10271 7 | THE MARIGOLD FIELD | *Diane Pearson* £1.25 |
| ☐ 10414 0 | SARAH WHITMAN | *Diane Pearson* £1.50 |
| ☐ 09462 5 | LAKELAND VET | *Joyce Stranger* 70p |
| ☐ 09891 4 | CHIA THE WILD CAT | *Joyce Stranger* 70p |
| ☐ 09893 0 | BREED OF GIANTS | *Joyce Stranger* 85p |
| ☐ 09892 2 | ZARA | *Joyce Stranger* 80p |

CORGI BOOKS, Cash Sales Department, P.O. Box 11 Falmouth, Cornwall.
Please send cheque or postal order, no currency.

U.K. Please allow 30p for the first book, 15p for the second book and 12p
for each additional book ordered to a maximum charge of £1.29

B.F.P.O. & EIRE allow 30p for the first book, 15p for the second book
plus 12p per copy for the next 7 books, thereafter 6p per book.

Overseas customers. Please allow 50p for the first book plus 15p per copy
for each additional book.

NAME (black letters) _____

ADDRESS _____

(SEPTEMBER 1980) _____